OUTSIDE THE ASYLUM

OUTSIDE THE ASYLUM

THE BEST NEW FICTION
2012

EDITED BY
MICHAEL STEWART

Grist Books 2011

Editor Michael Stewart

Cover Design Mark Savage

Inner Page Design Carnegie Publishing Ltd

Judges of the Grist Short Story Competition Helen Simpson
Mark Ellis Michael Stewart

Outside The Asylum is published by Grist Books.

Please note that all the work published here is previously
unpublished.

www.hud.ac.uk/grist

Grist Books is supported entirely by The University of
Huddersfield and would not exist without this support. We would
like to take the opportunity to express our gratitude for this
continuing support.

ISBN: 978-0-9563099-1-4

University of
HUDDERSFIELD
Inspiring tomorrow's professionals

ABOUT GRIST

Grist provides a unique platform for emerging writers.
By publishing emerging writers alongside some of the
best known names in literature, Grist offers a unique
opportunity for those starting out in their writing
careers.

THE WINNERS OF THE GRIST SHORT STORY COMPETITION – 2010

1st – Alexander McQueen on Your Birthday

Wes Lee

2nd – Slow Dance With a Skeleton

William Thirsk-Gaskill

3rd – A Crack

Tania Spooner

FOREWORD

Outside the Asylum is the name for the inside-out house featured in Douglas Adams's *So Long And Thanks For All The Fish*. The house was built by Wonko the Sane, after reading the instructions on a packet of toothpicks. When you enter the house you are leaving the asylum. Therefore, outside the asylum is the inside of the house. The asylum is everything else.

Outside the Asylum is a collection of the best new short fiction now. It features 26 original short stories from established and emerging writers. These stories form around a single theme: that of dramatising *in extremis personae*. By its brevity, short fiction often focuses on one character, in one situation, isolated and adrift from others.

Outside the Asylum celebrates the fragmentary and the partial in short fiction.

CONTENTS

Chloe

JENNY OLIVER

D EAR SUE,
I have been so caught up with my new polycarbonate greenhouse on the allotment, that other thoughts have been put to one side. Today I remembered an earlier conversation between us with some interest. As I told you, I had several children who died, maybe half a dozen, it's hard to recollect exactly. There is one I failed to mention and indeed only remembered today. She was a dismal creature, wailed and bawled frightfully, rattled her cot and rocked a lot.

In the end I put her in a cupboard under the stairs. The door was thick and fast, and after a while I scarcely heard her cries, and indeed forgot about her. Today I thought to take a look and there she is. She is very quiet, completely covered in filth, and crawling. I put her in the shower and left her there for some hours to loosen the mess, and covered her with Nivea. She is odd to look at after all this time. Strange eyes she has and no language – none with glottal stops – the sounds she makes are very fluid.

It was as much as I could do to wrest her from her cage, which might make good storage space when it's spruced up a bit. When Chloe – I have named her Chloe – her original name is past recall – when Chloe had been in the shower for some hours I observed that she needed feeding up, and could be of any age, for sure I don't remember. She makes no movements to speak of. I shall have to shower her for most of every day, at least a week, to get down to un-caked skin.

She took a little cranberry juice, but doesn't seem hungry. Now she is curled up with Benji by the fire. He seems to accept her, and before I left for work she was actually moving her fingers on his long hair, and looking at him (I think). She has been in the dark for so long I don't know if she has sight or can distinguish one thing from another.

I have not yet told Lesley about my discovery. Perhaps the greenhouse is the place for Chloe? What will I *do* with her Sue, *how* can I be a parent at my age?

Well duty calls,

Love Jenny

PS– Matty might do the cupboard?

Dear Sue,

I think 'parent' is not the word. She is very self-orientated, she may be autistic? She doesn't rest her gaze or 'look'. Except maybe that once with Benji. I think Benji can be her parent. He's willing to share his cushion, which must be a good sign. I shall be an onlooker and see what manifests. The word parent with regard to Chloe disturbs me, still I am interested, and that must count for something. Don't think I'll mention her to the social services. They might ask how she came to be in the cupboard in the first place. At least she doesn't moan, well of course that's *why* she had to be in there.

I can't stand moaning.

Love Jen x

Dear Sue,

Today I took Chloe to the greenhouse in a barrow. I have cut off all her hair with scissors.

It was very long and dank. She seemed to feel the feeling of cutting hair and was sort of listening I would say. Her face is extraordinary, unaware, and yet every touch of the scissors appears, visibly, reverberating through her to her toes. Maybe she's just not used to it yet.

I haven't tried to dress her, the business of arm holes and knickers, well, it just can't be done. Although in herself she looks far from dangerous. I am, believe it or not, treading very carefully. Lifting her into the barrow was like touching something untouchable, like spiders or snakes, or octopi, but it had to be done. She offered no resistance. She seems to sense any touch in her entirety, and almost ripples.

I covered her up in an old coat, and she sat on a cushion. She is much cleaner and fresher today. The Nivea seems to help, mother always swore by it. With her number one haircut I am sure she must be more comfortable. At the allotment I lifted her onto the bed that's dug over ready for the beans. I was longing to put her in the circular bed where the sweet peas are going.

Am I in danger of making a toy of her, a mascot? There is a level in her gaze that says to me 'you fucking dare', however where I put her, there she stays. Have to go now, there's shopping to be done. By the way, she hasn't eaten anything, though she did lift a clod of soil up to her mouth. I didn't like to stop her, it was almost slow motion, disquieting.

Bye for now,

    Jenny

Dear Sue,

Well this is a strange do. After three nights work I am often an insomniac and it's fine to sleep in front of the fire at any old time of the day or night. I'll speed up now, we must be getting on.

I came back from the Co-op with my shopping. I had left Chloe with her clod. The prospect of taking her naked to the shops in a barrow covered with an old coat was too complex. Besides, she has kept her own company for so long, she must be used to it, grateful even.

She has moved some distance when I come through the gate. She is standing, tall as I am, holding a white mooli radish with leafy greens. She walks awkwardly in my direction. I feel hollow and light-headed. Her eyes are water clear, she holds my look.

I am sitting on a white plastic garden chair in spotting rain, holding a white mooli radish. The earth around its stubby roots rubs off roughly with the first sharp tasting earthy bite.

Alexander McQueen on Your Birthday

WES LEE

Y OU THINK ABOUT him hanging from a cold stainless
rail in his wardrobe. The jolt that passed through
when you read the date. You think about his kilts, his
fierce otherworldly dresses, his ginger hair, *a ginge like
you*. You think about tartan, about his friend Vivienne
Westwood, the great old ruin, *another ginge*, she would
never kill herself, and if she did it would be in grand
old Dame style at ninety in her own bed. She'd send
out cards, not sympathy, playful tartan-covered cards
announcing her demise.

You think about Damien Hirst. Sniff the slippery
underbelly of his desultory shark. Slide around the eye-
holes of his diamond encrusted skull. Dismiss him quick,
another in no danger of killing himself.

You think about a woman you read about who overdosed between her pink satin sheets. A rich old American
heiress. When she turned forty she retired to bed, con-
ducted her life from her pink satin boudoir, then died
there. You remember the forensic photograph of her

propped up against her pillows wearing a purple silk eye mask, a large black Bakelite phone sunk into the middle of the bedspread, and a small caramel dog with a pink bow tied in its hair sunk in deeper, the way only warm flesh can sink.

You wonder if other famous people have killed themselves on your birthday. You don't care if they're famous, it's the other ones you want to think about, but you don't get to hear about them, you don't know their names, nobody does, you only ever get to think about the famous ones.

You think about the woman who took 60 painstakingly hoarded sleeping pills on Mother's Day. She passed out on the carpet and her dog ate her nose and lips. You type: *dog lips woman* into *Spotlight* to find that article – nothing comes up. You must have filed it under something else, something poetic, allusive. You add in: *floor* and *carpet* – nothing still. You think about the woman but you can't remember any more details, only that she lived. She had a face transplant and the donor was a woman who had hanged herself.

You think about Styal prison – on Mother's Day weekend, 41 women tried to take their lives.

You remember reading that suicide shouldn't be reported, that deaths sometimes occur after they appear in the newspaper. You think how faintly ridiculous this is. You wonder how many people took their lives after reading the article about not reporting suicide.

You think about how dates are so important. You remember the prisoner who escaped three consecutive years on May 13. He saw it as his lucky day because something great happened for him then when he was young. You think about how feelings get attached to dates, the way you remember May 13, that it was an unlucky day for you and always has been.

You fall asleep on the couch, dream you are walking through the rooms of your house. There is a body hanging somewhere. You'll find it in the master bedroom or out in the barn, but there is no barn. You wake at 3am, remember what someone told you: *when you dream of rooms you are dreaming about yourself.*

You pour yourself three fingers of bourbon, drop two ice cubes in your glass.

You think about the Victorians, how they used to bury suicides at a crossroads at midnight with a stake through the heart. The relatives would take a different route back home so the shade would be confused if it tried to follow them. You think about the fear, the shame that drove that stake, to pin the loved one to the ground.

You pour yourself another drink.

You find the article about the *dog eats lips woman*, jot down some details on a pad: *only knew there was something wrong when she tried to light a cigarette and it kept falling out of her mouth... they put the dog down... perhaps they are like sharks once they taste human flesh...* You had wondered what kind of dog it was but they didn't say.

You had planned to do a series of paintings on the hanging woman, the one who gave her face unknowingly.

You sift through yellowing piles of newsprint, find the chalk sketches you made, trace your fingers over the wintery lines: pale sides of beef, dismal hanging meat, the dread look in her eyes.

You feel the hairs rise over the back of your neck. You think about Mark Rothko's eyes – an image you have buried in your files – one of the last photographs of him ever taken: thick black glasses dwarfing his face, a terrified look in his eyes like a vaudeville performer just about to go on. What he felt that afternoon in his studio when he took a Stanley knife, slashed his throat and arms. It is the arms that haunt you, he slashed his shoulders so deep.

You think about Marilyn Monroe, *a ginge under platinum,* what she said after she was revived, one of the last times she overdosed: 'Alive. Too bad.'

And the photograph of her standing waving in a jeep in Korea after serenading the troops, the sun in her hair, looking like she was pure light. She had written on the back, 'I like this one the best.'

That *one day* when she was bathed in light.

You think about May 13, about the psych nurse, what you told her when you came round.

You think about your paintings, what it cost each time, to rape and beat your own body, throw it down a bank. How many times you've watched it tumble, roll out into the black road, stood there in the dark smoking a cigarette as a truck roared over it. You think you must be addicted to the feeling. Miraculously you get up and do it all over again.

You think about other artists, you always think about them. All the ones who suffer and stay. You admire their balls, their toughness, the way they still keep living. You admire the ones who live, but love the ones who die.

You think about your birthday.

How dates can become so important, like talismans, when everything is just random, things to hold onto in the roaring force of the world. You think about how a date can save you, the power of a number, the power of anything you have made up with your mind. You think about curves and squiggly lines and dashes and dots.

You think about Alexander McQueen.

That living is such a tenuous thing.

You consider the ice in your glass. Swirl it around. Things have always turned on a dime.

Slow Dance
With a Skeleton

WILLIAM THIRSK-GASKILL

I HAVE JUST finished compiling my ad for the personal
column in *Private Eye*. It reads like this:

> *Renaissance man, 27, 5' 10", clean-shaven, finan-*
> *cially solvent, seeks Renaissance woman. Good*
> *body (any size) desirable. Good intellect essential.*
> *Non-smoker preferred. No Christians.*

Private Eye has the most expensive personal column of
any journal I have come across, but I am persuaded that
this is because it gets the best replies. Money is no object
at the moment. I am placing this ad with no expectations
in mind: I just want to see what will happen. I don't care
whether the consequences are good or bad, as long as
they are interesting and unusual.

The ad contains one tiny element of misrepresenta-
tion: I am not 27 yet: I am 26 (my birthday is in a few
weeks). The world has no use for young, single, straight
men – certainly not in peacetime.

* * *

The ad was published last week, and I have had one reply so far, from a 23 year-old woman in Liverpool, called April. She sounds intelligent and educated, but I hope she is more interesting in person than she conveys in her letter. She likes early music and detective stories. I am now in the executive lounge at York railway station, waiting for a train to Liverpool Lime Street that leaves in two hours. The first class carriage on the trans-Pennine train is tiny and definitely not worth the extra expense, but I can easily afford it.

It is 11am and I am drinking free tea and coffee while I try to do *The Times* crossword. In between bursts of concentration, I am looking around at my fellow travellers, of whom I am delighted to say there are not many. There are a couple of businessmen who were having an irritatingly loud conversation about prospects in Kuwait, but this fortunately ended when one of them had to get up to catch his train. There is an elderly, genteel-looking couple, and a very striking-looking woman who is reading a magazine and sitting on her own. She looks about six feet tall, and has bright red hair and very white skin. Her hair has been forced somehow through a kind of black cylinder, which looks as if it might be made of ebony. The plume of hair sticks up at the back of her head like the flare from a bright red firework. She is wearing what I would call 'goth boots', which are heavy, leather, platform-soled, and decorated with metal plates. Her dress is black, and mostly concealed under her midnight purple, leather overcoat. She wears an assortment of metal rings in her ears and on her fingers. She is looking with a mixture of sarcastic amusement and harsh disapproval at whatever she is reading. Every so often, she emits a loud guffaw and takes a sip from the cup of black coffee which I noticed earlier she laced with something from a stainless steel flask she keeps in her capacious shoulder bag.

I get up, ostensibly to refill my cup from the machine at the back of the room, and I deliberately choose my route to enable me to glance down at what the red-haired woman is reading. It is *Private Eye*, and I am almost certain she had turned to the small ads pages. I am trying to think of something to say to her, but my mind is a complete blank.

Back in my seat, I start to wonder whether she has noticed me. She has definitely noticed me now, because she is holding up the hip flask in plain view and she mouths the words, 'Want some?' She looks at me with an expression that is quizzical and challenging rather than welcoming. I pick up my cup and my belongings, and go and sit in the chair next to her.

She holds the neck of the flask poised above my cup, which is less than half full.

'Yes, please,' I say, without a moment's hesitation. She obliges with a generous slug which produces coffee-flavoured vodka rather than vodka-flavoured coffee. I sip it, and am pleasantly surprised by the smoothness of the mixture. I take two more sips. I take a mouthful. It goes down easily. I take another mouthful. I drain the cup. I want some more. She holds the open flask upside down and shakes it gently from side-to-side in a gesture of defeat.

'Shall I get some more?' I ask her. She looks at me with disdain.

'Do you mean the stuff from the mini-mart in the station? Mm – yummy! It'd be better than meths, I suppose.'

'Back in a few minutes,' I tell her as I get up.

I walk out of the main exit from the station and, there being no queue at the rank, I get straight into the first taxi. I take a short ride to 'Oddbins', buy a bottle of 'Bison Grass' Polish vodka, and return within fifteen minutes. I have the crumpled receipt in my pocket but, without looking at it, I have no idea how much the bottle of vodka cost.

'I was just beginning to get worried,' she calmly informs me as I sit down again in the same chair as before. In spite of herself, her face lights up for a moment as I produce the bottle. She refills her hip flask, without spilling a drop. We discreetly keep the bottle in its bag, and have another round of stiff vodka-coffees.

'What's your name?' she asks. I don't respond immediately. 'Is that a difficult question?' she continues.

'Harold.'

'Harold?' she sniggers. She throws her head back, closes her eyes, and laughs silently but almost uncontrollably. When she recovers herself, she is almost out of breath. 'You don't look like a "Harold",' she explains, as if that makes everything all right.

'What would you say a "Harold" looks like? Do you want me to stick an arrow in my eye?'

'Good one!' We chink our cups together in a moment of harmonious celebration. She gives me a sidelong glance, and studies me for a moment. I am expecting her to say something, but nothing happens. She returns to her magazine. There being nothing better to do, I go back to my crossword and pour another shot of vodka into my cup.

'Ha!' she exclaims. 'Look at this sad boy.' She reads from the advertisement on the page in front of her.

> *'Just what the world needs: another twenty-some-thing single man. Cambridge-educated, sensitive, inexperienced, based in West London. Seeks*

interesting and understanding woman for serious
relationship with a view to marriage.'

'He sounds all right,' I protest. And then I think, why am I advocating on behalf of another, straight, male advertiser?

'He sounds like a little lost boy who's going to come to a bad end,' she insists.

'And look at this pretentious twat.' She reads my carefully composed effort, in its entirety. 'Why is it so vitally important that he's clean-shaven?' she asks.

'A lot of women don't like beards.' She looks blank.

'And why does he say he's financially solvent?'

'Wouldn't you object to a partner who is saddled with debt?'

'Would you?'

'I think I would, yes.'

'Why are you seemingly so interested in me, then?'

'Are you telling me that you are saddled with debt?'

She pauses before replying.

'No comment.' Another pause. 'That's you, isn't it?'

'What?'

'That advertisement – you placed it, didn't you?'

'Yes.' She laughs again, more uproariously than before.

'I'm six feet tall, and twenty-eight years old. I could *never* have anything to do with a man who was either shorter or younger than me.'

* * *

An hour later, I am on the phone to April, giving her an excuse about a fictitious grandmother who has been suddenly taken ill. I am not going to Liverpool any more, I have been back to the ticket office and am now going to

Edinburgh with a tall red-headed goth whose name I still don't know.

* * *

Her name, as far as I know, is 'Cassandra'. That is what she told me. She told me a lot of other things. What I mean is that a lot of other things came out of her mouth. Whether 'she' was saying them is something that I don't understand.

This is our third night in The Scotsman hotel in Edinburgh. Everything is being charged to one of my credit cards. I honestly cannot tell you at this point whether the limit on the card has been blown or not.

I am sitting on the floor in the bathroom with a bottle of whisky, my notebook and a pen. I am writing down what has happened. Don't ask me why I am writing it down. I just don't know what else to do. I probably should be doing something, but I don't know what.

Cassandra is having the latest in a series of what I would call 'psychotic episodes'. Our first night here was blissful. The second night was weird, verging on scary. All I will say about today is that, the moment Cassandra is physically capable of getting the lift down the lobby, we are leaving. I hardly slept, but discovered this morning that she had doodled and coloured and written random words and phrases all over the bedside telephone with a biro. One of the things she put was 'Please help me'.

Cassandra started telling me her life story and previous relationships. To begin with, it was conversational, pleasant, and interesting. We had drinks in the bar. We had dinner. We had another drink after dinner. We moved upstairs, by which point Cassandra had begun to attract attention because of her outbursts and her behaviour.

I did not actually push her into the lift, but I certainly wanted to.

This is what Cassandra said, as closely as I can remember.

'I had a boyfriend called Simon. He was the only man I have ever loved. He was gentle and kind and very sensitive. We used to take drugs together. All I ever took was cannabis and speed, but Simon did other things. Our dealer was another goth called Hilary. I always made fun of him because he had a girl's name. He hates me. I tried to get Simon to hold back on what he was taking, but I failed. Hilary sold him something which killed him. I will never forgive Hilary for that, and I will never forgive myself, either. I threatened to tell the police. Ever since, Hilary has been trying to destroy me. He has keys to my house which I think he took off Simon's body when he was dead. He and his crew let themselves in, and they do things like erasing files on my computer, listening to my answer phone, even cooking and leaving the kitchen in a mess – anything to ram it down my throat that my living space is not my own. He also takes my bank card and draws money out of my account. I am about a thousand pounds overdrawn at the moment because of his stealing from me. Hilary got his girlfriend to impersonate me, and they took out a personal loan in my name.'

Don't ask me why she did not get the locks changed, or talk to the bank about the fraudulent transactions, or to the police about the drug-dealing. Don't ask me why she does not seek treatment for her mental illness.

* * *

I cannot remember how we got back to Cassandra's house.

We had a passably content few weeks, spent mostly in Cassandra's house, which is a rented Victorian terrace. She then started to go down again, and has now been sitting almost unmoving for three days with the curtains closed. Her house is untidy, cluttered and smells of stale incense. She has many prints on the walls: Dali, Bosch, Klimt, Edward Hopper. She has four cats, whom I have had to look after while she has been ill. I hate animals but I felt sorry for them. She has shelves full of books and vinyl records, most of which have been thoroughly clawed by the cats.

I have cleared the ornaments, brass incense-burners, candlesticks, boxes full of spent matches, jewellery cases, vases of dead flowers, records with no covers, books, and cat hairs off the table, and I have written a letter to Cassandra.

My Dearest Cassandra,

You are the most beautiful, captivating, intelligent, fascinating woman I have ever met, or ever expect to meet – when you are rational and not depressed. Unfortunately, I now realise that that is not enough to sustain us.

I cannot live the way you do. If the house were to catch fire, I would call the fire brigade and then get on with the rest of my life. You wouldn't. You say that all I do is call the fire brigade because it's not my house and I don't understand what a fire is like. While we argue, the house burns down. Have you noticed how, after one of our rows has been going on for hours, we move off the original subject and instead have an argument about the argument itself? You say you have a lot of problems, which is true. What you do not say is that most of your problems are capable of solution – some of them by fairly simple means.

The thing I cannot stand about you is the way you allow yourself to be tormented by Hilary. Since you let slip where he lived, every day I have considered going round to his house with an iron bar. You have messed with my sense of justice, you have taken my money, and you have started to erode my sanity. I am now going to walk to York station, and get on a train. That train will take me to the next episode in my life, but you won't be on it.

Love, Harold.

I left the letter on the table, picked up my bag, let myself out quietly, and walked to the station. I was sitting on a bench on the platform, when my phone rang.

I went back to Cassandra's house. Eleven years later, after our divorce, I finally caught the train.

A Crack

TANIA SPOONER

H E A S K E D I F she would like to go and see the giant crack at the Tate Modern, his thin voice far away down the end of a land-line.

'What crack? How on earth?'

'I guess in the floor of the Turbine hall?' he said.

She felt immediately adamant. They must have put a fake crack in a fake floor then. It is an old and revered power station. She pictured the straight, indestructible contours of that building and wondered, 'how else?'

But constructing the raised floor, in her mind, and digging the crack into it, she failed to see what all the excitement was about – with all the real cracks being made in the world – and for the rest of the week she stayed bothered. Of all the installations in all the world, why was he taking her to see a crack? Was he trying to lure her towards what he would not speak? She called to find out. Days had passed, and her phone started beeping as soon as he picked up. When the interruptions began sounding rude and deliberate, she apologised for her handset, which was running out of battery.

'I don't mind the beeps,' he said, before ranting about how he had spent a whole day on the phone to BT, listening to repeated recordings and endless muzak, whilst trying to reach an operator who would register his new number. It was a boring conversation, she thought. Amusing herself, she pretended that BT had engineered the beeps, to censor their unspoken profanities. When the beeps accelerated to an almost seismic pulse, she imagined a swearing place that neither of them could access. Beeps from the deep crack, she was thinking.

I don't think I can do this, he wanted to say.

Talking to a friend who understood elements, she was told she was being too negative, that she should try being more positive. Here was a plan her boyfriend had initiated. She could support his maleness by taking a step back, allowing him to make the calls. If it was something he wanted, she should allow the distance between their lives to be sealed in quiet.

It was suggested she try chanting: to the green Tara who was born of a single tear of Avalokiteshvara.

It was suggested she go see the woman who hugs.

'Yes. Go. Go,' her friend said. 'To Crystal Palace. Stay overnight. It's amazing. She is pure love. It is everything we need.'

'Where do you sleep?' she asked her friend.

'Just go. Go. Everyone just goes to be there.'

'Will I have to queue up for a hug?'

When she thought of being hugged, she thought of needing to lie down. She would curl up on the floor underneath a long-standing line of people, all chatting about feeling the love.

'I'm sure it's sold out already?'

'No, there's no advance booking,' her friend said, 'the whole thing is a queue. The whole point is that anyone can go, and she treats everyone the same.'

'Does she speak to you?' She wouldn't go unless the woman could speak.

'Yes, in your ear when she gives you the hug,' the friend said.

And of course that's it, isn't it? Deep into the ear. That's the place. Beep beep. The crack to fall into.

On the phone the next time, after he had called and she could only cry, he whispered, 'I am back. I am here. You *are* in my heart.'

They held onto their phones, like doctors with stethoscopes, and listened to one another's breathing.

I am the cat dropped in a wheelie bin, she did not say.

On Friday, she went to the Portobello market to hang out with a friend who had a stall there.

'When you fill your heart with Krishna in the morning,' her friend said, 'everything gets better.'

They were standing at her friend's rag and bone cart. Intermittently, the friend shouted, 'come on darlings, fill your bag for a fiver.' As the people in the crowd drew closer, she thought she saw them blush to see a woman who can juggle sexy and sounding like a fish-wife.

In amongst the heap of clothing on the cart, among the nylon slips and the stale blouses, was a man's sweater, a senior-citizen stiffness to it. Holding it up by its odd arms, one shrunken, stout, the other mangled but dangling loose, the elastic pulled out, she said, 'You can sell this?'

'Oh yeah,' her friend said, winking, and kicking at a cardboard box with her white trainer. She was always pulling her jeans up at the back, to stop them falling down.

A young man was drifting through the crowd, banging a tuppeny drum. He was reborn, in all-white robes, a pale tangerine scarf, and she decided that his feet were especially well-cared for, inside their yellow, hand-knitted socks, and fluorescent-orange shoes. All at once and with her head thrown back, her friend let out an ebullient cackle. Her breasts were jiggling, her hoop earrings were shaking like a tambourine. The young man turned his face towards them and smiled.

At the same time, the sun appeared over the dark rooftops. The way the sunshine was slanted, slamming down upon her eyelids, she stepped to the side and into the shadows. Of course, she thought, who wants a shadow, if you can have something more cheerful, like her friend here. If she were only that shiny and plump with happiness, wouldn't her boyfriend want to see her much, much, more?

Of course, wanting to see him all the time only made her seem desperate. If she took notice of the women-who-have-everything, she should try wanting him less. It was quite easy to think of things she didn't like. After their first date, she had to stop herself from looking down at his shoes, and judging his ox-blood Doc Marten's too wide for his skinny legs. More recently, his chunky shoulders were an irritation, when she was trying to cook, and they blocked her from the fridge. But, as it happened, she scolded herself. If she really meant to love this man wouldn't she try loving his burgundy T-shirts?

He admitted that it must be difficult to be the person making the suggestions all the time. When she had looked exasperated, he had said, 'I'm afraid there probably isn't much point in going out with me.'

'But there is a point,' she had insisted, even if he could not always see it. Looking into his gentle eyes, she said that she would see it for the two of them. When they lay together in bed, she was steadied by his focus, his almost feline sensitivity. She liked to feel herself close to his porcelain-white, smooth and almost hairless skin. She felt grateful for the real 3D-ness of his embrace when he pulled her more tightly into his arms. It was only at weekends that she yearned for him to want her more. On crisp autumn Sundays, that she searched for ways to cheer him up.

'Thing is, you need to tell him that you really want to see him.'

'Cook him dinner.'

This: the advice of married friends who lived in a forest.

'He pulls away if I want him too much.' She might have felt embarrassed to lay her feelings bare. But these friends were generous people, with whom hanging out was made so easy, that pretty much everything she thought came spilling out.

'He doesn't like pressure of any kind. I'm not even allowed to know for sure whether we're spending Christmas together.'

'I'd go mad not knowing that,' the wife said, getting up to grab more food from the pan on the cooker.

She turned to see her friend using her hands to spoon more roast parsnips and potatoes onto their plates.

'He doesn't like it when I go mad, you see,' she said, falling silent. It was the vision she had of her boyfriend blowing apart like a dandelion clock. He hates upset. Would punish a single puff of irate female madness. Phffffwwww – he loves you, she thought. Phffffwwww – he loves you not. Or, Phffffwwww – he loves you at one o'clock, for that is as far as it would go.

'All women go mad once a month,' the husband said opening a second, tall, bottle of his own homemade cider.

There had been a harvest full moon, the weekend they stayed at a boutique hotel. She had not been able to sleep. The reading light woke him. Then, a conversation in the wee hours, about the 'extras' on the bill, set him off. He started worrying again, about his work and all the financial pressures. She lay rigid on her side of the bed,

23

contrite, watching him dress. He left the room without saying anything, before it was even light outside. When he still hadn't come back and it was nearly nine o' clock, she went to get herself breakfast.

She walked into the dining room alone, and immediately took a seat at a table with a sea view. The waiter came over and offered to clear away the opposite placement. He asked if she was alone and she hesitated to answer. Instead, she asked him if she could borrow a spare pen. The waiter took away the other glass, the side plate and the spare cutlery, and she took out her notebook and began writing down her feelings, getting them out on paper. Later, looking across the room, she watched as the waiter showed a pair of burly-looking men to a table for four people. Soon afterwards, the blokes were joined by their obliging girlfriends, both blonde and sitting down at the seat opposite their thick-set part-ners. The waiter hovered over the couples, preparing to take their orders. He began speaking in a showy-offy, stand-up sort of way, as if he meant to be heard across the room.

'She thinks she's Agatha Christie, I saw a TV pro-gramme about Agatha Christie once. She might be a famous writer, but she was a terrible wife, you know.'

When she left the hotel to go down to the beach, she was carrying a china cup and saucer in her handbag. Standing on the narrow boardwalk, away from the fishermen, she raised both her arms and hurled the hotel china into the sea. The tide was out and there were rocks under the shallow waters. Her aim was direct, and both the cup and the saucer shat-tered. Kaleidoscopic broken pieces settled like a loose jigsaw. The dark sea-bed became patterned with white. Pretty, she thought, slumping down, her back against the sea wall. She was listening to the lapping waves, close to her toes, when suddenly he was standing above her. He was looking past her down into the water. They were unmistakable: shards of smashed crockery. He said it was a shame to damage sea-life, that he was worried now for the sea-creatures.

'He says he loses the connection when I get mad,' she said, 'I suggested counselling, to help us communicate better, but he says he doesn't want to do anything I suggest anymore.'

'So what does he want?' the married couple chimed.

'To go see the crack at the Tate,' she said.

And the next time she spoke to her boyfriend she said, 'I'll go and see the giant crack at the Tate, tomorrow, if that's what you'd like?'

It is 4000 miles to the centre of the earth, they say.

She rose up the escalator from the underground, and noticing a gleam on the steel vaulted ceiling, she began praying. She prayed for everything to be ok, for her boyfriend to be there. And he was. He was waiting for her in fact, just inside the glass doors, standing next to a guard where the hot air from the vents rushed at their faces.

'Let's try, let's walk the crack,' she said.

It wasn't immediately clear where to go to find the artwork. It didn't stand out like the huge spider had, or the giant sunarama, and there were no signs pointing them to it. Instead, it was lying as if unintentionally, and somewhat ignored, existing without fuss, in the floor. At first glance, it remained unclear, why this giant fissure in the concrete floor of a majestic building? All she could think about was the artist in conversation with the curator, asking: if you don't mind I'd like to bang a hole in your foundations, cut a rip through your polished concrete floor.

He was more interested to know how the crack was really made. Kneeling down together, they peered inside the rent and found a whole other world of industry.

Pointing to the tiny chicken-wire meshing inside the crack, he traced his palm along the inner walls, along the miniature moulded canyons, appreciating the painstaking care and detail of the construction.

Then, hand-in-hand, and walking carefully, they followed the zigzag path of the chasm, knowing people had fallen in and broken their arms and legs.

She also noticed how many other couples had come to see the crack. In front of them now, two gay men, enjoying a photo opportunity, and they stood watching as one of the men lowered himself into a sitting position, cross-legged, his crack over the big crack. The boyfriend who had been taking the photos then swapped places and, kneeling down on the floor, rolled up his sleeve and ventured an arm down into the deepest part of the crack. Whilst looking up at the camera, he leant backwards, grimacing and making out he was trying to release an arm that had got stuck.

Her own boyfriend laughed at this. He laughed, in that way that made her want to get inside his warm chuckling, baggy sweater.

'It's like the crack is sucking him in,' he laughed.

It wasn't until they were at the far end of the Turbine Hall, where the crack fizzled into the smallest thread, that they started hugging, and holding onto one other. At first, she thought she was holding him, but then it felt more like he was holding her, in his large hands. Standing, double-buttressed and leaning into one another for a long time, they could both feel it, how they wanted to love and be loved. Both their legs were shaking, and when it felt like they would never be able to stand up alone again, they pulled apart.

Walking away, she held her boyfriend's arm, feeling his muscle, the bone in his shoulder, sliding her feet and enjoying the smoothness and cement of the floor.

Earth: A Review

STEVEN MAXWELL

S INCE ITS INSTALMENT nine months ago, the Earth has been the museum's most popular exhibit. The Earth, approximately the size of a delivery van and spotlit by a concentrated 10,000 watt sunlamp, revolves in the heart of an enormous black room in London's Science Museum. It hangs suspended, as if by wire, in such a fragile way you think the whole thing may suddenly topple, its oceans spilling forth in torrents, drowning and crushing you simultaneously. Unlike anything ever seen before, not only in the art world but also in the science world, the Earth brings a whole new meaning to the term 'performance art'. 'Look close...' urges the sign (but not too close, as one elderly woman from Brighton discovered when her head bounded off the beachball-sized crescent moon orbiting the Earth), and when you do, peering through one of the twelve purpose-built magnification units encircling the glowing sphere, what you see is nothing short of astonishing.

Oceans breathing in and out, fizzing across shorelines. Electrical storms flashing within swirling cloud mass. Ships scratching the royal blue seas with foamy white ticks. Pine-fresh forests releasing aromas that call up Christmas time. Molten veins streaking across volcanic ridges like subterraneous forked lightning. Steamy jungles, smelling of pond water and frogs, emitting watery warbling. Amorphous desert regions shifting in constant flux. Ozone emanating from the atmosphere – that exquisite blue skin – reeking of frizzled fuses and scorched phosphorus. And even after all these wonders (plus more, so much more) the Earth turns its page to night and unveils a lacework of intricately sparkling cityscapes that shiver in the moonshine like raindrops on cobwebs.

As with any masterwork, visitors have reported an array of responses to the Earth. Young couples love its plump radiance, feeling it somehow represents the limitless potential of their blooming romance, while married couples affectionately recall looking around their own planet and drinking in its marvels: blazing sunsets, frothing waterfalls, summer lightning, hazy rainbows, wind-hewn landscapes. Some have said they see the Earth as a gift, a second chance to nurture something beautiful, and a powerful reminder of the lack of respect we have for our own planet; while others, doomily, suspect it to be a harbinger foretelling ecological disaster. Unsurprisingly, Greenpeace are petitioning for full ownership of the spinning spherical sensation. And then there's the case of the fourteen-year-old girl who has begun a campaign to free the Earth and return it to its natural habitat after spotting 'scared and vulnerable' denizens of the miniature replica scrabbling across its surface into buildings and caves and beneath trees, seeking shelter from the looming, sky-filling faces. But the curator of the exhibit is said to be disregarding the girl's campaign for one very valid reason: he has no idea where the Earth's natural habitat is.

He claims the Earth simply appeared one morning in the car park of the museum, levitating soundlessly in a shipping container stamped with that ageless maxim: HANDLE WITH CARE. Upon opening the container and discovering its wondrous contents, the curator immediately closed off or placed into storage every exhibition in the museum to give the Earth maximum multimedia exposure. Regardless of any negative feedback (which, admittedly, is minimal), the curator is delighted by the fervent excitement the Earth has generated.

But now, in the wake of three damning reports appearing in the international press, everyone is talking about the Earth and questioning if it is indeed hostile, dangerous. First was the American student attacked by 'tiny rockets' after plunging her arm elbow-deep into the warm waters of the Pacific to retrieve a pencil. Then came the Chinese dendrologist claiming he was also attacked by missiles after plucking the Earth's largest living tree, a giant sequoia named General Sherman in California's Sequoia National Park, as a 'souvenir'. And then came perhaps the most damaging of all the reports from the museum's own head caretaker, who said one morning he had to scoop up micro jetliners and Earth-orbiting satellites that had torn free of their gravitational field and crash-landed on the polished black floor 'like dandruff'. He said he used the museum's microscopes to look for any identifiable country markings, then checked Google Earth to find where to return them, but when entering the Earth's atmosphere he had to be quick as 'those tiny rockets they've got trained on us, they're quick to use them'. The caretaker then rolled up his sleeve to reveal a brawny forearm peppered in what looked like dozens of cigarette burns.

Despite all three of these people having since reported diarrhoea, nausea, vomiting, and hair-loss, there doesn't appear to be any governing body willing to shut down the exhibition on the grounds of potential radiation sickness. Indeed, the curator himself has waved off these claims as 'outlandish' and 'mere coincidence'.

Of the hundreds of world-renowned scientists who have studied the Earth only four have stepped up to pronounce its legitimacy, though all have been somewhat reticent to propose any explanatory theories regarding origin or meaning, the two obvious questions at the forefront of the debate. So is it a parallel world detached from its moorings? Have we invaded its space or has it invaded ours? Is it a future echo of ourselves? Did it pass through a wormhole, a black-hole, time itself? Is it extremely small or are we extremely large? These questions have sent every scientist, theologian, philosopher, and poet back to their proverbial drawing boards. Physics alone, in all of its variations (nucleonics, astrophysics, quantum mechanics, etc), is understandably being rethought and rewritten at this very moment. But given that the sign on the door simply reads 'Earth: anon. contribution', what is the most common question from the visitors? Naturally it is, 'Who is the artist?'

The curator remains optimistic that the artist, the creator of the Earth, will come forward with another masterwork, perhaps a teeming alien planet or even Heaven itself. In fact, he has already begun creating space.

A Perfectly Ordinary Man

BEN CHEETHAM

S IGHING, M AX PUT the sheaf of technical drawings down. It was no good, his eyes were too tired
to focus. The Luftwaffe planes had pried their way into
his dreams again, flight after flight of them, droning end-
lessly overhead. Eventually, he'd given up on sleep and
gone downstairs to sit by the living-room window, glass
of wine in hand, his gaze fixed on the distant glow of
the chimneys that never stopped smoking. Shortly after
dawn, his wife, Anna, came bustling into the room, furi-
ously wielding a duster.

'Look at all this dust,' she said, attacking the contents
of the mantelpiece. 'Just look at it, Max.' She picked a
cushion off the sofa and hit it with the flat of her hand,
sending a puff of dust into Max's face. As he took his
glasses off and polished them on his shirtsleeve, she
looked around the living-room with a slightly frantic
widening of her eyes. 'Clean, clean and clean. Sweep,
mop, dust. Wash the walls, beat the rugs. That's all I do
these days, but anyone visiting would think the house
hadn't been cleaned in a year.'

From upstairs a child's voice called, 'Mummy, mummy.'

Anna didn't seem to hear it. She rubbed fiercely at a sideboard with her cloth. 'I never open the windows, not even a crack, but still it gets in somehow. It's ruining everything. The curtains, the bed-linen, our clothes-'

'Anna,' interrupted Max, 'Martin's calling you.'

She paused from her dusting, frowning at the ceiling.

'Go and see what he wants.'

'I'll be late getting into the factory.'

'But it's only just after seven.'

'I promised to go in early today.' Anna's frown intensified.

'That's the second time this week. I hope they're paying you for all this extra work.' Max's eyes blinked away from hers, and she made a humphing noise. 'You shouldn't let them take advantage of you, Max.'

'I don't.'

'Oh yes you do. They walk all over you, and you just take it.'

'Mummy,' the cry came again, more urgent than before.

'I'd better see what he wants,' said Max, hurrying from the room. As he climbed the stairs, he released a heavy breath that was part relief, part weariness.

A boy of about ten years old was stood in his pyjamas on the landing, his face flushed and tear-streaked. A wet patch stretched from his groin down the legs of his pyjama bottoms.

'It's happened again,' he said, sniffling back a sob.

'Oh dear. Never mind, nothing to worry about. Come on, let's get you cleaned up.' Max ushered Martin into the bathroom. He set a bath running, while Martin undressed. Once Martin was in the bath, Max gathered up the pyjamas and took them to Anna.

'I can't believe it, not again,' she said, examining them as though they were evidence from a crime. 'This is the third time this week.' She heaved a sigh. 'I'm beginning to think we should try a different approach. If you ask me, we've been giving him too much attention when what he really needs is discipline.'

Max looked doubtful.

'If we suddenly go getting all tough on him, it might make things worse.'

Anna dismissed his words with a flick of her hand.

'A good dose of discipline never did anyone any harm. He won't like it. There'll be tears for sure. But I'd rather that than see him end up like–' She broke off, pressing her lips together to keep from saying anything more.

'End up like what?' said Max, a flush rising up his neck. 'Like me?'

Anna flinched from Max's gaze. He looked over her shoulder at the mirror above the mantelpiece. A bespectacled man of forty, with tired blue eyes and a soft, pale face – the face of someone who wouldn't hurt a fly, as his mother always used to say – stared back. A splinter of irritation worked its way into his mind at the sight. He rearranged his features into what he judged to be a stern, hard-eyed expression.

'Okay, Anna. We'll try it your way.'

Without waiting for her response, he made his way back upstairs. Martin was lying in the bath, staring dreamily at the ceiling. 'What are you doing still in the bath, for heaven's sake?' snapped Max.

Flinching at the unfamiliar harshness of his father's tone, Martin clambered out of the bath. 'Come on, slow coach, quicker, quicker,' urged Max. 'You've got five minutes to get yourself dry, get your school clothes on, and brush your teeth and hair, or there's going to be trouble.'

Martin pulled on his trousers, stuffing both legs into the same hole in his haste. He looked to Max for help, but none was forthcoming. Tears bubbled into his eyes. 'There's no point turning on the waterworks,' said Max, folding his arms. 'We've done too much for you, that's the problem here. Well, from now on things are going to be different. You're nearly eleven...' His voice faltered. Tears were rolling down Martin's cheeks, his bottom lip was quivering. Max's expression softened for a second, then grew severe again. 'It's time you started to do more for yourself, instead of relying on us for every little thing.' He tapped his wristwatch. 'Three minutes. If you're not ready and sat at the kitchen table in three minutes, they'll be no breakfast for you this morning.'

Max left the bathroom. Martin's shuddering sobs followed him all the way downstairs. The sound was like a hand reaching inside him to squeeze his stomach. He could barely keep the resentment from his voice as he told Anna what the sobs were about. She nodded in approval.

'Well, it's a start.'

'I've got to get going to work. I'll see you later.'

'Don't I get a kiss goodbye?' asked Anna as Max started to turn away. Reluctantly, he stooped to give her a cold peck. 'Oh don't be like that, Max,' she said. 'This is for the best.'

I'll believe that when I see it, Max felt like retorting, but instead he forced a thin little smile and kept quiet. Anna fetched his coat, wiping the dust from it before handing it to him. 'And remember what I said, Max, you mustn't let them take advantage. You must have confidence in your abilities. You're the best engineer they've got, and you deserve to be rewarded for all the hard work you put in. If they won't pay you what you're worth, there are dozens of other companies that will.'

Max nodded without much conviction. At the front door, he paused to glance at his watch. Five minutes was up and there was no sign of Martin. Sighing inwardly, he picked up his briefcase and left the house.

When Max got home from work an hour late, he knew something was wrong the instant he stepped through the front door. The house was too quiet. Anna was sat staring at the kitchen table. She barely gave him a glance as he entered the room.

'How was your day?' she asked, from force of habit.

'Exhausting.' Max breathed the word out in a long rush of air. 'How about yours?'

Anna gave a slight shrug, drawing an aimless pattern in the whitish-grey flakes of dust with her finger.

'You know, when you look at it, it's actually quite beautiful. Almost like snow.'

'Where's Martin?'

'I sent him to bed early. He had another one of his little accidents at school today.'

Feeling a knot tighten in his stomach, Max glanced at the ceiling.

'Maybe I should go see him, make sure he's –'

'No,' cut in Anna. 'Leave him be. He's got to learn that from now on, every time it happens he'll be punished for it.'

Surely it's punishment enough that he was humiliated at school, thought Max. But he said nothing. Anna took his dinner out of the oven and put it on the table in front of him. He ate mechanically, not really tasting his food, swilling it down with wine. He always drank a glass of wine with his evening meal, but recently one glass had turned into three or four – a fact that hadn't escaped Anna's disapproving notice. 'You shouldn't drink so fast, darling,' she said, as he reached for the already half-empty bottle. 'It's not good for you.'

'Neither is doing a job where I'm unappreciated and underpaid, yet I still get up and go into work every day.'

Anna eyed Max knowingly. 'You didn't speak to them, did you?'

'Yes I spoke to them, but they were too busy to listen.'

Air hissed through Anna's teeth.

'They're always too busy.'

'Of course they are, and I'll tell you why. Inefficiency. They need a more efficient product. And I could give them it.' Max pulled some papers out of his briefcase and waved them at Anna. His voice rose to an angry pitch he could never have attained without half a bottle under his belt. 'But why should I, eh? Why should I?'

Max slammed the papers onto the table, stood and stomped from the kitchen. His footsteps grew lighter as he ascended the stairs. He stood listening outside Martin's bedroom. When he caught a low sound of sniffling, a pained look came into his eyes. His hand moved reflexively towards the door handle, then stopped. Fingers curling into a fist, he wrenched it back and forced himself to walk into the bathroom. After washing the stink of the day off, he returned downstairs.

Anna was in the living room now, his papers spread over her lap.

'How is he?' she asked, looking up at him with narrowed eyes.

Max shrugged.

'I didn't go in to see him. If we're going to do this, we might as well do it right.'

The lines around Anna's eyes relaxed a little. She even managed a smile, before lowering her head to resume studying the papers.

'So, what do you think of my design?' asked Max.

'It looks interesting. But what is it exactly?'

'I call it The Continuous-Operation Corpse Incineration Oven for Mass Use.'

'That's a bit of a mouthful.'

'I know. I need to come up with a snappier name.'

'How does it work?'

Max picked up a technical drawing of what appeared to be a four-storey building with a staircase running from the first floor to a hole in the roof.

'The corpses are loaded in there.' He pointed at the hole and began to trace a path downward. 'They slide on slanted grates from one storey to the next, being heated and then set on fire by the corpses already burning below.' As always when discussing a project that excited him, Max grew increasingly animated, his eyes gleamed and his voice quickened. 'And that's the real beauty of my design. Not only does it have the capacity to burn thousands upon thousands of bodies per day, but once the oven's fully heated the bodies themselves fuel its operation.'

'Sounds like the perfect solution to all their problems, but are you sure it would actually work?'

'Sure I'm sure! My oven would be ten times more efficient even than the five-oven crematorium we installed at Auschwitz last year.' A wrinkle of doubt creased Max's forehead. 'The only thing I'm worried about is that corpse parts might stick on the grates and clog the oven.'

'Have you shown these drawings to anyone else?'

'Not yet.'

'Good. We need to think carefully about what to do.' Anna tapped the papers. 'This could really make your name. What we don't want is for one of the chief engineers to get their claws on it, make some minor alteration or other and then claim all the credit for themselves.'

Heaving a sigh, Max pushed his glasses up to massage his eyes. 'You look exhausted,' said Anna.

'I'm so tired I can hardly think. I haven't slept properly in months, what with work and Martin and those damn planes.'

Anna reached out to stroke Max's arm.

'Let's go to bed, sleep on this. We can talk about it again in the morning.'

Max nodded. Anna took his hand, led him upstairs and helped him undress as though he was a child. He lay down and took a deep breath. The air smelled stale from the windows having been closed for so long. *Like a tomb*, he thought. His body buzzed with tiredness, but even so he couldn't sleep. So many thoughts whirled through his mind, so many frustrations, fears, hopes. One hour passed. Two hours. Anna snored beside him. He began to feel suffocated. The air seemed to be getting thicker and harder to breathe. Heart pounding, he rose quickly, pulled on his dressing gown and left the room. A sound brought him to a halt by Martin's bedroom door – it was the intermittent snuffle of tears. He reached for the door handle, hesitated, then grasped it and pushed. Martin was sat up in bed, head in hands, elbows on knees. His whole body trembled from the effort of stifling his sobs. It hurt Max to his core to see him like that.

When Max sat on the edge of the bed, Martin lifted his head and asked,

'What's wrong with me, daddy?'

'There's nothing wrong with you, you're a perfectly normal boy.'

'So why do I keep having my accidents?'

'It's like the doctor said. It's just a phase, something you'll outgrow. Now you lie back and close your eyes. That's it,' soothed Max. Stroking Martin's hair, he murmured over and over, 'Everything's going to be alright. Everything's going to be alright.' He listened as Martin's breathing slowed into sleep. Then he kissed his forehead, tiptoed from the room and made his way downstairs in search of the unfinished bottle of wine. He released a sigh as the wine eased through him, gazing out the window at the hellish yellow-orange glow away in the distance, beyond the factory.

Entirely Useless Monument

CHRISTIAN STRETTON

E DWARD TALKED ABOUT his plans for the Entirely Useless Monument long before he actually began working on it. He had been playing around with the idea for a while.

'The plan is,' he would explain, 'to build a structure from only natural materials in my back garden. It should have no function apart from an aesthetic one, and it should be large, much taller than me – as big as the house if possible. I would work on it for one year, and when the year is up, whatever the condition of the structure, then the Monument will be finished.

At this stage (which Edward would later refer to as the Planning Stage) reactions were overwhelmingly positive. 'Good for you,' people would intone. They would even offer suggestions of what they thought the Monument should look like: It should have feathers, it should represent the different stages of your life, it should be hollow, you should be able to climb it.

Edward was a creative person, though this was not reflected in his career trajectory. Following a series of clashes with the teachers, Edward had quit college at the age of seventeen, and being too proud to live off his parents' substantial income, he had immediately found a well paid but dull position in a bank. In this job he had worked quietly and conscientiously, slowly rising in the company to his current position as a middle-manager.

When work actually got started on the Monument, reactions were more mixed. The next-door neighbour was especially concerned. A keen member of the Residents' Association, her objections became quite vocal from the beginning. She was most concerned about the noise, and about the effect that the structure would have on house prices in the area. After all, the Monument would be in clear view from her window. Even Edward's family counselled against his decision.

Karl, his best friend from college, was absolutely behind him. He even helped with some of the preliminary sketches and loaned Edward the tools. So, in October 2009, work began in earnest, and soon there developed a clear pattern to Edward's week.

Wednesday: sketch the additions which were to be made this week. This would usually be done on bits of scrap paper during quiet periods in the bank.

Thursday: visit the local hardware shop on the way home from work to buy the necessary wood and materials needed.

Friday evening: sit in the garden with a beer, just contemplating the structure, and imagining the future possibilities (this was the highlight of Edward's week).

Saturday: lay out tools and building materials. Work for two hours in the morning, then stop for lunch. Sometimes, work would recommence in the afternoon, sometimes those two hours would be enough.

Sunday: bask in the glory of his work. Sometimes this would involve inviting friends around to the house to look at the Monument, sometimes it would simply involve feeling pleased with himself for the most part of the day.

Monday: nothing. Forget about the project.

Tuesday: an anxious feeling would enter his sub-conscious, always extant in the back of his mind. This creeping paranoia would not subside until Wednesday came around again, and Edward set back to work on the project.

He continued in this cycle for a whole year, and though the slump of Monday and Tuesday were a drag, the sheer exhilaration of the build on Saturday kept him focused. And because he had adhered to this weekly routine so stubbornly, the Monument had really taken shape.

On his final Saturday morning, Edward sanded some rough edges, then put down his electric sander, and stood back to take in the view. The Monument was now every-thing he had hoped for. It would be pointless to describe it here, but suffice to say that it now satisfied every par-ticular of Edward's original brief.

Even the next-door neighbour had to concede that it was quite a spectacle. People from all over the town came to visit the neighbourhood just to sneak a peek at the majesty of it. The Entirely Useless Monument was a hit.

Karl would sometimes ask Edward what was next:

'We could add a wing to the side of it, and a dome. A dome would be awesome.'

But for Edward, this was missing the point.

'You don't understand,' he would reply. 'It's finished.'

The Man Who Never Grew Up

HOLLY ORESCHNICK

O NCE UPON A time, in a land much like our own,
lived a very sad and lonely old man. This old man
had no friends at all because he had to keep travelling
from village to village, carrying just a few belongings in
an old tattered sack. Just as the old man had started to
settle down in a village and begin to make friends, something would go wrong and people would begin to be
mean to the poor old man and so he would have to run
away and begin his life again. The old man found it ever
so hard to make friends in each new village, he wasn't
anything like the other grown-ups he would meet. He
found grown-ups terribly boring, they either just sat and
talked about boring facts and figures or were terribly serious about silly things like money and marriages. The old
man was not like this at all. The old man saw too much
beauty in the world to talk to the boring grown-ups who
were no longer interested in the important things in life.
The old man had a secret that he told no one, he didn't
feel like a grown-up at all, in his heart he felt like a child.

Now this may sound like a very funny thing to say
of such an old man, and he was a very old man at 72,

45

but what this old man enjoyed more than anything was having a good tickle fight or a game of tag or even sometimes hide and seek. But no grown-up would play these games with him, they thought that only children played these games and it was strange to want to play them at 72. So one day, as the old man walked into a new village he decided he knew what he had to do: he had to make friends with a child.

But how was he to make friends with a child? Surely children would just see him as an old man and say, 'No, I won't play with you, you are a grown-up and are too boring for me to play with!' and run away before he could tell them he wasn't a grown-up at all. So as he approached a new village he decided he would make something that children would love so much that they just had to like him too. He decided to make a teddy bear.

The old man sat in his little room and began to make the bear by firelight. The old man told the bear all about his secret and why he was making him. He told him about how grown-ups didn't understand him and how lonely he felt. He told the bear all about how he wished he was still a child and could play games again and have friends and didn't have to be lonely anymore. When the bear was finished the old man held him up to the light.

'I will call you Bear,' he said. He knew it wasn't a terribly interesting name but he decided it would have to do.

Bear was born knowing the beauty of children, he knew all about their laughs, their little chubby cheeks and hands and even their mischievous nature. Bear was born loving children just as much as the old man did. The old man even made Bear a little stool opposite the door so when children came in Bear would be the first thing they saw. Bear was very excited about this and tried to wait patiently for a child to come and play.

A week after Bear was finished the old man decided it was time for him to try and make friends with a child so one day he decided to wait outside of a school to see if he could meet someone. At the end of the day all the children came running out of the school, some holding pictures and crafts they had made, others just their school books, one very raucous boy came out holding nothing at all and was sent back in by his daddy to go and get his satchel. The old man felt very happy watching the children but soon they began to disappear back home with their parents before he had even had a chance to talk to them. How sad the old man felt then. And Bear would be ever so disappointed. But just then, one lonely child, a young girl who looked about six or seven, came out of the school. No other parents were around and the girl looked very, very sad.

'I know,' thought the old man, 'I'll take her back to my house and we can play before she has to go home.'

The old man got up and went to the school gate where the little girl now stood. She was ever so pretty and had long, dark hair almost down to her bottom, half hanging out of a ponytail.

'Are you alone?' he asked the girl.

She nodded.

'How about coming back to my house and we can play? I've got a lovely teddy bear who would love to meet you. You can call me uncle.' He added.

The girl looked up at the kind old man and even though she knew she shouldn't talk to strangers decided that as he was so old and kind looking he couldn't possibly be mean or scary and must be someone she could trust, so slipped her sticky hand in his, after all her mummy wasn't there so she had nowhere else to go.

The old man was amazed. The child didn't look at him like a grown-up at all. She didn't presume he was a boring man or concerned about silly things, instead she held his hand as if they had been friends forever.

'Would you like a sweet?' he asked.

The girl beamed at the old man and took the sweet, happily sucking it and skipping as they walked.

'Now you know what you can call me, but what do I call you?' he asked as they walked up the road together, her mummy still nowhere in sight.

'Wendy,' she answered.

'Well Wendy, let's go and have fun then.'

The old man held her hand tight and they began to run, giggling as the wind beat against their faces. As they got to the old man's room and opened the door, Bear looked up and didn't just see the old man as he had been expecting, but saw Wendy too. Wendy ran over to Bear and picked him up. She held him ever so close to her chest and gave him a big, big hug.

'What's his name?' she asked.

'Bear,' said the old man.

'Hello Bear,' she said.

Wendy sat herself down on the floor and chatted to Bear, the old man sat down on his chair and watched.

'Why don't you come here and show me Bear?' he said tapping his knee.

Wendy trotted over and plonked herself on his knee and began to kiss Bear. Bear looked up at Wendy with glee. He could smell her soft, powdery skin and laid back sighing with joy at such a sweet scent. Each of her kisses he memorised so he could never forget them. Bear knew now why the old man loved children so much. Wendy was the most charming thing he had ever seen.

'Are you ticklish?' the old man asked. Wendy squealed in anticipation.

'I think you are!' he said.

Bear felt very happy that the old man could play again and cuddled into Wendy hearing both their giggles. But the old man must have been very tired because he started breathing rather heavily whilst he was tickling Wendy, but still he carried on. Suddenly Wendy tried to wiggle out of the old man's arms but he kept her tight on his knee.

'Don't you want to play anymore?' the old man said to her, tickling the top part of her leg.

Wendy burst into tears and threw Bear across the room. Poor Bear hurt his paw rather badly and could not understand why Wendy had hurt him so. When Bear looked up, the old man looked sad too and Bear desperately wanted to comfort him. The old man whispered in Wendy's ear and told her to stop crying and be a good girl for uncle. She sniffed a few times and nodded. The old man let go of her and she calmed down.

'Better go find mummy,' she said.

'Mind what I've said now,' the old man replied as Wendy got to the door.

After she left the old man walked over to Bear and picked him up.

'Some children can be a little naughty,' he said, 'But I think she's good deep down, don't be too sad, I'm sure she'll be our friend.'

Bear cuddled into the old man and thanked him for being so kind. The old man popped Bear back down on his chair and went and stood by the window looking lonelier than ever.

The old man and Bear didn't see Wendy at all for another week but one day, as the old man and Bear were looking out of the window watching a girl skip, Bear recognised Wendy sat on the pavement. The girl skipping was a pretty blonde thing but she was not a very kind person. In fact, just as Bear and the old man saw Wendy, she too spotted her and with each skip she called her a new horrid name. The old man left Bear in the window and went to the door.

'Wendy!' he called, 'Do you want to come in?'

Wendy's eyes looked terribly red as if she had been crying. Bear wanted to cuddle her and make her feel better and was no longer cross at her for hurting his paw.

Wendy stood up and the mean girl asked Wendy where she was going and called her more names and said she was running away like a sissy.

'She is coming to play with her uncle instead of with mean, ugly girls like you,' the old man said.

Wendy grinned and stuck her tongue out at the blonde girl.

Bear sat up very straight and tried to look as friendly and lovely as possible and as Wendy came into the room she asked where Bear was and when the old man pointed to the window he had left Bear sitting in, she ran over to it and hugged him really tight.

'Sorry Bear,' she said and kissed him on the head.

Bear forgave her and cuddled her back.

'How about a game then?' the old man said to Wendy. Bear grinned, he liked playing games nearly as much as the old man did.

Wendy thought for a second and then said,

'Not tickling,'

The old man nodded, thought and said, 'I know! Let's play hide and seek, I haven't played it in years, I'll count!' The old man looked very excited and Wendy ran off with Bear to hide. The old man only lived in a tiny room so there wasn't many places to hide but Wendy saw the bed with a big heavy duvet on top and leapt under it.

'You have to be quiet Bear and hold your breath otherwise he'll find us!' she whispered.

From across the room they could hear the old man reaching the count of ten. It was terribly exciting and Bear held his breath tight and tried not to move at all. The old man began to look around the room.

'Are you behind here?' he called as he pulled back the curtains. 'Or under here?' he said, looking under the chair. Just as he walked towards the bed and was about to pull the covers off there was a knock at the door. 'Oh fiddlesticks,' said the old man, 'it was just getting fun!'

Wendy peeped out of the duvet covers and watched the old man walk to the door and when he opened it, how shocked she was to see her mummy standing there. Wendy began to worry she must be in terrible trouble and hid again so her mummy wouldn't see her as she looked ever so cross.

'Where's my daughter?' her mummy asked.

'Oh I'm terribly sorry,' the old man said, 'I saw your daughter was rather upset because a girl was picking on her so I invited her in until she went away so she could get home safely to you.'

Wendy's mummy looked a little confused as she hadn't met the old man before and she wasn't used to people being so kind. 'I was only trying to help,' the old man said, looking rather sheepish.

'Oh I'm sorry sir, thank you. Wendy come along now!' Wendy got out of bed and tucked Bear in under the covers, 'Thank the kind gentleman,' her mummy said.

'Thank you,' said Wendy, 'Bye Bear!'

Bear tried to wave but his paws were tucked in too tight.

'I'm free anytime to mind her if you need it,' the old man said. Wendy's mummy thanked him again and took

Wendy away. Bear thought that the old man was so kind for taking care of Wendy and hoped that her mummy would let them look after her. Although the old man looked sad that Wendy had gone he also felt happy as now it looked like they would be able to be friends after all.

The old man started enjoying living in this new village and hoped he would never have to move again. Wendy's mummy had told everyone what a lovely, lonely gentleman he was and so people started talking to him in the shops and other children began to play with him and call him Uncle as well. People brought him soup and casseroles and offered to come and clean for him. It really began to look like he was fitting in. The old man and Bear were very happy and felt like they were really going to live happily ever after. But the old man began to miss Wendy terribly because he had not seen her in a long time. He would sit and talk to Bear about how much he loved her and how he missed her sweet little face. No other child was as good as Wendy and if another child came to the house to play, somehow it just didn't feel the same.

'I love her,' the old man said to Bear one day, 'and I wish she could be here always and always so we could play together every day.'

Even though the old man now had lots and lots of friends, a lot of whom were children, he began to feel lonely and sad again. Bear began sitting in the window hoping Wendy would pass, see him and come in. But of all the children he saw walking by the window, Wendy was not one of them.

'I know what we have to do!' exclaimed the old man, 'we must find Wendy and run away together. I know she *must* miss me too. And then we can be together always!'

Bear felt he could jump up and down with glee. A life with Wendy would be a life of happiness. So the old man approached Wendy's mummy and asked if he could pick Wendy up some time from school as he missed her charming little face. The old man was so loved in the village Wendy's mummy immediately said yes and the old man came back to his house a very happy man.

'Now, we must make sure we have everything she could need,' he said, packing his few belongings.

That day he went to the small town and brought Wendy all sorts of clothes and pretty things. He filled his pockets with sweets and even got her a special drink to help her sleep so she could rest on the journey. Bear was terribly excited and couldn't wait until the following afternoon when they would go and pick Wendy up from school.

The morning of the journey the old man made sure everything was packed and made lots and lots of sandwiches with all sorts of lovely fillings, jam and honey and even chocolate spread.

'Wendy must have the best!' he said.

Bear too began to prepare himself, practising looking happy, looking sad – just in case he wanted an extra cuddle – and how to look like he was ready for a jolly good time.

At three o'clock Bear and the old man set out to the school, leaving the luggage at the house to pick up later. Wendy seemed happier today and Bear and the old man agreed she must be very excited to see them. As Wendy came up to the old man she slipped her hand in his and the old man was as excited as a schoolboy.

'Let's go home,' the old man said to Wendy. He handed her Bear and she held his paw as they walked along.

At the house the old man made Wendy an extra special hot chocolate with the sleeping drink in it so she would be ready for the journey.

'Drink up Wendy,' he said, stroking her hair.

Soon Wendy began to feel ever so sleepy and asked if she could take a nap. The old man carried her to his bed, stripped her down to her knickers and popped her under the covers and gave her Bear to cuddle.

'I'm sleepy too,' the old man said, undressing and getting into bed next to her.

Wendy was soon fast asleep cuddling Bear into her chest. Bear could hear the old man breathing heavily again and was happy he was having a little rest as he sounded ever so tired. Bear thought it was just wonderful for the three of them to be cuddled up so cosily and he too began to fall asleep. But then, Bear suddenly fell out of bed. Bear tried to cry out and find out what had happened but he couldn't see onto the bed from the floor, he was too small. After a little while, the old man got out of bed, smelling a little funny and saw Bear on the floor.

'Sorry Bear,' he said, 'I got a little excited there, didn't mean to knock you off.' He picked bear up and popped him next to Wendy who wasn't under the covers anymore. Bear cuddled into Wendy and there they slept whilst the old man got ready for the journey up ahead.

Half an hour later he dressed the sleeping Wendy and draped her over his shoulder. He popped Bear into his pocket and picked up the bags and locked the door for the last time. It was time to leave the village.

Just twenty minutes later Wendy's mummy arrived at the old man's door to pick Wendy up and found she was not there. As the old man walked into the countryside Bear wondered why he could hear sirens in the distance. He shut his eyes and fell asleep ready to start their new adventure and, of course, to live happily ever after.

Imitating
Catherine Walker

ALEXEI SAYLE

R ory suddenly realised it had been over a month and Catherine Walker hadn't had her period yet, so obviously he needed to buy some Tampax for her. At lunchtime he got the bus right across to West London and bought an overpriced box in a Korean supermarket. When he got back to Catherine's room he opened the box and left it open on her bedside table: she would not be the sort of girl who'd hide such things away. Then the thought struck him, why would she leave a full box open on her bedside table? So he had to take some out; but then immediately another thought struck him, how many of these things did women get through in a... what would you call it, 'a session'?

In the end, after much thought, he removed four of the things from the box then rode another bus right across to East London and left them in four separate litter bins. This took a considerable time since litter bins – unlike massive piles of litter – were few and far between right across East London.

When Rory got back to his flat it was late, he hadn't got any work done and he'd spent most of the day carrying tampons around on public transport. Rory sat on the couch, put his head in his hands and wondered how he'd got into this situation. Where could you say it had started to go wrong? Six weeks ago he certainly hadn't felt like this, a month and a half ago he'd been optimistic and happy with a feeling that he was finally getting back on his feet after so many hard times.

From 1984 to the mid 90s he'd been a wealthy man, often appearing on 'The Money Programme', or 'Channel 4 News', being interviewed about the massively successful business that he owned called 'The Classic Car Phone Company'. At the time when he'd had the idea for it he'd been a small-time publisher and the owner of one of the very first car phones, its bulky works built into the boot of his MG Montego. It had occurred to Rory one day that people who owned classic cars like E-Type Jaguars, Gullwing Mercedes SLs, Bentley Coupes, Porsche 356s, were forced to have the same mobile phones as everyone else, their angular modern 80s plastic lines clashing with the more curvaceous, leather and wood-clad interiors of their vehicles. Rory's inspiration was to begin manufacturing a range of car phones that matched the insides of these classic cars: Bakelite handsets in place of plastic, chromed dials in place of push buttons, cloth wire in place of black cable. Soon the business expanded and he was making all kinds of things that didn't look like themselves: personal computers disguised as spindly Regency writing desks, CCTV cameras built into wrought iron lanterns to guard the gateways of converted Victorian warehouses and gilt rococo microwave cookers for the kitchens of Jewish homes in North London.

All was well until the internet boom of the late 90s. Making the mistake of thinking (as many powerful people do) that because he was good at *one* thing he was good at *every* thing, Rory invested all his money and some that wasn't his in a website called 'mybum.com'. Now when he reflected on it he couldn't properly recall exactly what service 'mybum.com' purported to offer the internet user. Indeed now he wasn't entirely sure that anybody involved had the slightest idea what it was the site was supposed to do, apart from produce money like a mountain spring just by dint of it being a website. This supposition turned out not to be true.

His partner Jenny had taken the bankruptcy and the loss of their home quite hard but she had never openly blamed him for his idiotic greed and he was grateful for that. When they managed to obtain the tiny two bed-roomed housing association flat on a quiet street south of King's Cross she stopped crying all the time and occasionally even managed a shy smile.

This tranquil period lasted until Byron and Danuta came to stay. Byron had been Rory's closest friend at university but while Rory had gone into business Byron never settled. Rory liked to think of the other man as his wilder alter ego, travelling the world, living with the Mud Men of Papua New Guinea, getting into fights in a bar in Vietnam, being the gigolo of an aged poetess in Helsinki. For the last four years, according to the occasional curt email, he had been working in Somalia for a Spanish medical charity called 'Medicos Sin Sombreros' (Doctors Without Hats) but over a fizzing phone line from Mogadishu Byron had yelled, 'Rory mate I'm coming back to London, OK to crash for a while at your place?'

'Of course mate,' replied Rory. 'You know we don't have the money we once had, I mean the spare room is pretty small but yeah sure... '

'Don't worry. The old lady'll be cool?'

'The old lady'll be well cool.'

'Great mate, see you next Tuesday then.'

During the intervening period between the phone call and Byron's arrival Rory spent many hours daydreaming about what it would be like to have his closest friend living with him. When they greeted Byron at the arrivals gate at Heathrow carrying a big funny sign saying 'Lord Byron' they found he had brought back with him from Somalia, a tropical disease which made him a ghastly yellow colour, six very big suitcases and an extremely bad-tempered Croatian woman called Danuta.

As Rory's battered Volvo estate turned into their street they passed on the left a little petting zoo attached to a children's playground, behind whose iron railings over-indulged sheep grazed.

'What sort of sheep are those?' asked Danuta, who'd been silent the whole length of the A40, from the passenger seat.

'Ooh, I don't really know,' said Jenny.

Danuta swore in Croatian then said mockingly, 'Dey don't know what sheep it is dat live round de corner from dem... dey are idiots not to know what kind of sheep it is.'

'So what kind are they Danuta?' asked Rory in a friendly, enquiring voice.

'I don't fucking know!' she shouted, 'but then they aren't my fucking sheep are they you cretin?'

'I was only...' stuttered Rory before Byron cut across him.

'Hey just lay off her mate alright? She's had a tough time OK?'

'Yeah, sure, I'm sorry,' said Rory, aware that Jenny in the back seat was giving him a look which implied he was a weak-willed weasel even though he could only see one of her eyes under the enormous suitcase that was slowly crushing her.

As soon as they arrived Byron and Danuta immediately went to bed in the spare room where they had a noisy argument followed by very noisy sex while Rory and Jenny hauled their suitcases up the four flights of stairs.

The two travellers emerged at one in the morning, woke their hosts up and forced them to cook a huge meal which they ate without stopping smoking. Byron and Danuta had brought with them twenty cartons of a brand of Somalian cigarettes called 'Monkey Priest' which they smoked constantly, so that acrid grey clouds soon hung in the kitchen like low mist over a swamp.

Over the meal Byron told them, food spilling from his mouth, how everything was better in Somalia and how the lives of Rory and Jenny lacked spirituality, then he read them extracts from his poetry and showed them drawings he'd done of Danuta seen from the back, kneeling exposed and naked with her behind up in the air.

During the next couple of weeks Rory and Jenny endured strange smells in their toilet, violent arguments between their guests followed by even more violent making up and a deluge of insults from Danuta concerning their ignorance of different types of sheep until one day Jenny suddenly said, 'Rory I can't take any more of this.'

'I know darling,' he replied. 'I'll see to it.'

'Byron mate,' Rory said when the couple got back from the swimming baths, 'sorry but we need the spare room back. Catherine Walker, Jenny's best mate from school's coming to stay, she's just split up with her boyfriend so you know...'

Rory had been expecting some strong resistance from Byron but rather sweetly his best friend said, 'Sure mate, if the chick's in trouble. Me and Danu will check into one of those bed and breakfast places in Argyle Square. Only thing is I'll have to leave our suitcases in the spare room 'cos I'll need to get at my poems and notebooks, change of clothes and stuff.'

Rory was so relieved at Byron's easy acquiescence that he readily agreed to him leaving his luggage behind. It took him a while to realise that if Byron was going to be visiting the spare room often then he would have to fake Catherine Walker's presence in that room.

At first he approached this task with enthusiasm: he got some Prada shoes Jenny had bought at Milan airport that were far too small for her and threw them on the floor, he got the two red silk Agent Provocateur bra and pants sets his partner had always refused to have any-thing to do with and lay them on a chair, he found a small stylish leather suitcase left over from their wealthy days at the back of their wardrobe and put in it other T-shirts, jeans and tops that Jenny had grown too fat to wear. Then he happily stood back to look at his work and felt immediately deflated; he realised it was surprisingly difficult to get a sense of somebody's absent presence. At the moment it was just an empty room with some stuff in it, there was no hint of Catherine Walker's personality.

He went into the living room and took down 'Anna Karenina' (a book he'd always meant to read) from the bookshelf and laid it open at page forty-nine on the table beside the bed. Next he picked up a glass and half-filled it with water, got some old scarlet lipstick of Jen's from her makeup box and with a strange tingling sensa-tion in his calves smeared it on his own lips then took a sip and placed the glass also on the bedside table next to the book. Finally he sprayed the last of Jenny's 'Very Valentino' in the air. Again he stepped back and felt, with a deep sense of satisfaction that now Catherine Walker's personality was beginning to emerge. You could see that here was a bright, intelligent woman who wasn't afraid to look good. She liked sexy shoes, saucy underwear and vibrant lipstick. As he closed the door Rory felt a strong pang of regret that Catherine Walker wasn't really staying in their spare room.

'I see the chick's reading Tolstoy,' said Byron after his first visit to his luggage.

'That's right,' replied Rory, 'she's a really clever woman, good-looking too.'

'I'd love to know what she thinks about Anna.'

'I'll ask her mate.'

So Rory read the book lying in Catherine's bed wearing the cute pin-striped men's pyjamas that Catherine wore to sleep in and a few days later he went down to Leather Lane Market and bought Catherine some stylish designer knock-offs: three skimpy spaghetti-strap T shirts and a tight leather skirt that would show off her lovely little firm bottom. Rory felt a sudden stab of annoyance at Jenny. Why wasn't she more like Catherine? He thought, why didn't she wear sexy clothes and work out at the gym three times a week like the other woman did? Jenny really needed to pull herself together.

'She appreciates Tolstoy's ability in bringing Anna so vividly to life,' he told Byron on his second visit '... but ultimately she says she despises her for falling so hysterically in love with such a transparent bastard as Vronsky when her husband is actually a better more moral man. She says she'd never do anything like that, she's got too much self-respect.'

They then went on to discuss Catherine's sparkling academic record, the martial arts black belt she possessed and the affair she'd had with Lenny Kravitz. As the two old friends talked on into the evening it dawned on Rory that the awkwardness which had existed since Byron's return from Somalia vanished when they talked about Catherine Walker.

About a week later Byron suddenly asked.

'Do you think she's ever had sex with another woman?'

'Who Catherine?'

'Yeah.'

'I'll ask her,' said Rory, 'that's the thing – she's so upfront you can talk easily to her about stuff like that.'

'Yes she has,' Rory told Byron on his fifth visit. 'We had a bottle of wine together late the other night and she told me all about it. She likes men most. Her exact words were, she's "got to have a regular supply of dick", but a couple of times she's had crushes on women and you know... once or twice it's led to, well sex... kissing and fondling and rubbing and stuff... but no sex toys. She thinks that's unnatural.'

'Wow,' exhaled Byron with a far-away look in his eyes.

'Yeah wow,' said Rory. 'She told me the thing she noticed when you're like, kissing a woman is how small their mouths are, compared to men's.'

'Oh God,' said Byron, 'I have simply got to meet this woman.'

Sometimes I Think If I Start Crying Then I Aint Gonna Stop

MARK ELLIS

S o I sit down and order a pint of something and drink it. And the girl asks me if I want another so I say yeah and I start to drink that. And there's this guy sat at a table in the corner watching me. This big parrot sat on his shoulder: like a pirate but he's wearing charity shop cast-offs. You know – when people leave clothes in a bag on the doorstep and they're probably covered in shit? Clothes like that. The parrot isn't looking that good either, in fact, I'm not so sure if he isn't missing one of his eyes. He's got one toe left on his right foot and he kind of walks with this hop that he drives from his neck down through his body. And I'm sitting there watching him and he says to me, 'What the fuck are you looking at?'

So I look away and the next thing I know, the air's all wings and I've got this fucking parrot in front of me hopping around on the bar.

'What the fuck are you looking at?' he says.

'Nothing.' I say.

The parrot pecks at the bar then looks at me.

'You were watching us,' he says. 'Staring.'

I shrug and take a sip of my drink. In the corner, the man's just sitting there looking at me.

'Like we've got dicks on our faces.'

I go to stand up.

'You're all right,' I say.

'Fuck we are. Sit down, sit the fuck down.'

I hold up my hands.

'Sure. Look, I didn't mean anything by it you're...' The parrot cocks its head to the side. 'You don't see people with parrots. That's all. Not very often.'

'Or the other way.'

'Both ways,' I say.

'So you gonna buy us a drink then?' I look at the guy then back at the parrot.

'Both of you?'

The parrot squares up to me again so I beckon the girl over. The parrot wants Captain Morgan's and the man's drinking an Orange and Passionfruit J$_2$O.

'He's driving,' says the parrot.

'Sure.' I get them their drinks and another beer for myself.

The parrot tells me to take the drinks over. The parrot lands next to the glass of rum, picks it up with his beak and downs it. Then he drops the glass on the table and inhales slowly before turning to me and saying, 'Sit down.'

The man nods so I kick out a stool and join them. Just looking at each other. I'm drinking pretty fast but the parrot finishes first and calls to the girl behind the bar to bring us over another round. The man just sits there sipping his J_2O.

'I don't get it.' I say.

The parrot shuffles a little and the man looks up from his glass.

'What?' says the parrot. 'Don't get what?'

'It's like a joke,' I say. 'This is just like a fucking joke.'

He's got his feathers puffed up and he's coming for me across the table in my face and I've got my hands up to stop him pecking my eyes out. The man lets out this death rattle of a cough and the parrot stops and we both look at him. He swallows something down. The parrot comes back to me.

'You wanna know something funny? Eh? Something fucking hilarious?' He looks at the man again. 'There was this woman, yeah? Used to come in here quite a lot. Thought I was *real* cute. She used to sit where you're sitting, spend the whole day talking to us. Stories, you know? One day they just stopped her allowance, you know? Money for food and shit. She had a young girl. About thirteen or something. Never saw her again. Heard she was going out on the boats and fucking the sailors for a bit of cash. They all do it.' He looks at me and I nod. 'Anyway, word is that one of them had their way with her and then pushed her overboard. Gone.'

I look over at the man and he nods.

'I don't get it,' I say.

'Next thing you know her girl's doing the same and the same thing happens to her.' The parrot necks his drink. 'So that's both of them gone.'

'And they never caught who it was?'

'Never even bothered.'

The parrot leans forwards whispering in my ear.

'Sometimes... ' He swallows. 'Sometimes I think that if I let it get to me, if I let all this shit stick – sometimes I think that if I start crying – then I'm never, ever gonna be able to stop.' He turns away and goes back to his drink. Swallows it down. I order us another round.

Towards the Visceral

JACK MOSS

P HILIP LABOURN, SLOUCHED in his chair, let the voices blur out. Press interviews were always the worst part. Got him on edge. He'd done dozens by now, and still felt that little bit uncomfortable in front of a mic. Like they were trying to catch him out. Classic sign of success: always someone trying to pull you down.

Next to him, Mark Peterson leaned over, tested the microphone, and cleared his throat into it. The hubbub died down.

'Okay folks. It's great to see you all here today,' he said with a smile, 'Now I trust I don't need to remind you that Philip is only available for Q&A for the next thirty minutes. This session finishes at 3pm, so...'

He had to work hard to sound genuine in these bits. Bloody slog, that's what they were. Still, you can't write off the press, so to speak. They're the ones who make sure people are still mentioning you decades down the line. Best way to live forever is to keep people talking about you.

Born Philip Burn in 1981 in Dagenham, North East London, Labourn was a hugely successful and equally controversial visual artist, whose works were praised by his multitude of devoted followers as the most profound statement on the human condition ever put to canvas.

'... Anyway, enough of me,' Peterson was saying, 'Let me turn you over to Philip.'

Labourn straightened up and gave his best hollow smile to the assembled journalists. Give nothing away. Air of mystery and all that.

'Afternoon ladies and gentlemen,' he said through the smile, 'I won't waste your time with any preamble. Most of you should know how I go with these things, so let's hear your questions.'

'Much of your work has been very austere in hue, but this new exhibit is characterised by the use of the colour red,' someone said, 'Is this a shift towards more visceral, corporeal material?'

Straight off the bat. The journalist was young, fresh faced, leaning over his pad eagerly, speaking in carefully polished sentences. He'll have spent all last night on the wording of that one. They only speak in prose, this lot.

'So the question is, why have I started using red?' he asked, still smiling. Some of the others in the audience shared his smirk. The veterans, they'd seen him fuck about with the wide-eyed kids before.

'Erm ... more or less,' the youth said, forced to go off-script. He rallied, 'I mean ... colour is such an integral part of your composition, the power and energy of these pieces seems to feed from the hues employed. It gives such a different mood to this exhibit. How significant is this new choice of colour?'

'To be honest, mate,' Labourn shifted back in his chair, 'I used red because I'd ran out of grey.'

There were guffaws in the audience. It was all part of the game in a Philip Labourn interview – the pithy quotations, the piss-taking. The young journalist smiled weakly, scribbled something down. It's all irony, though. Right?

> *Throughout his career, Labourn was guarded over the workings of his creative process, although he often implied that random, uncoordinated creative spasms played a strong role in his techniques.*

'Next question,' Labourn ordered, enjoying himself a little bit now. He always felt better once he'd played a few of them for fools.

'Philip,' said another journalist. He recognised this one. Broadsheet writer, real pretentious twat. Thought he was on first name terms. 'With another exhibition opening, the inevitable critical debates over your work keep cropping up. How do you respond to those who have labelled your work a farce, or written it off as Dadaism?'

Dada – he was used to that word now. The first time a critic had dropped it on him all he could do was laugh and brush over it. After that occasion he had gone home and done his research – straight onto Wikipedia. Cheeky bastards. These days he was well prepared for that little slight, just you watch.

> *Labourn's popularity was far from universal, however, with some less sympathetic critics labelling him a mere peddler of reborn Dadaism. His followers would argue that his work takes art in a direction that Dada could only hint towards. His work has also been described as disrespectful*

towards canonical works and institutions of the
written word, another critique which may have
been said to have missed the point.

'People say I'm making Dada as though it's some sort of insult,' Labourn said, 'Where'd we be today without it, eh? All these chopped up sharks and bear costumes you've got winning the Turner Prize, and my work is the farce? Art's a farce, chum, has been for ages. If people single me out like that, to me it's saying this guy's jealous. He's probably studied art his whole life and he's never going to get to where I am. There's no such thing as Dada anymore. It's all just the same stuff.'

'Your newest work contains a lot of collage elements taken specifically from print journalism,' someone else asked, 'Is this an attempt to hit back at your critics?'

'I got bored of chopping up classic books,' Labourn said dismissively, 'There's all sorts in there. Politics, sport, crossword clues. It's all words at the end of the day. It's all material.'

'So would you say it's a holistic continuation, for want of a better term, with your older works?'

'That's up to you lot to decide,' Labourn replied, winking, 'I can't be giving you all the bloody answers, can I?'

Labourn's visual compositions are characterised by
their swirling, chaotic abstract panoramas, which
are overlaid by disjointed excerpts of written lan-
guage from many sources. Shakespeare, the Bible
and newspaper articles have all been interpo-
lated into Labourn's shattered visions. Recurring
throughout is the number 11 – the significance
of which was never directly revealed by Labourn
himself, who once remarked of it, in typically

brash and ironic style: 'Ambiguity is what pays the bills in this business'.

At just gone 3pm he stepped out of the warmth of the assembled print media into the open expanse of the main gallery hall. He breathed out, felt the cool air run over his close-cropped hair and opted against putting his leather jacket back on. Still too warm for art-wanker style right now. Sweat prickled on his neck after the interrogation. You got through it, mate. Survived another one and they're none the wiser.

It was quiet out in the gallery. The exhibit wouldn't open to the great unwashed until Monday, so the long hall was inhabited by only a few knots of press people, VIPs, gallery bigwigs and potential collectors already sniffing over the pickings. He didn't begrudge them. Neither did his wallet.

He scanned across the milling punters, searching. There was usually at least one. They always found tickets somewhere when he was attending in person. When he cottoned on, he started encouraging it. He had put tickets on his website for this appearance. Sometimes a random twat would get his hands on them first, but they sold so quickly you could bet money there'd be at least one there.

His gaze paused over a red-haired girl in the corner, looking at him. There you go. He could always tell straight off from the eyes. Looking at him like he was the fucking Messiah, or something. He ran his fingers through his goatee, making sure it was trimmed. Of course it was, he'd gone over it that morning with the clippers. Better put the jacket on now.

He strode across the marble floor, giving her a different smile to the one he'd gifted the critical hordes earlier. She was dressed in typical fashion. You can always tell the art students, because they try so hard to look like unique snowflakes. The pains he'd taken to fit in with them. The itchy facial hair for one. And this fucking jacket. He'd even changed his name, made it sound a bit French. Can't go wrong with French in these circles.

'Hi,' he said in a melodious tone, 'I'm Philip Labourn.'

'I know,' she said quickly, looking into his eyes with adulation, 'I know all about you and your work.'

Of course you do, love. You'll know a little bit more before long.

'Oh really?' he asked with practised surprise, 'It's always nice to meet a fan. What's your name?'

'Jamey,' she said, eyes to his.

'Nice to meet you, Jamey,' he said, 'Would you like a personal tour of the exhibit?'

Her pupils widened a little, 'Really? I'd love that.'

'Not a problem,' Labourn said, 'I'm always happy to oblige my fans.'

'Thank you,' she said.

He let her lead the way towards the first canvas, making sure to collect his due eyeful. Bloody hell. How many blokes would kill to pull the girls he had. It was the one thing to make this all goatee-leather-jacket-French-name shite worthwhile, otherwise he'd collect his cheque, thank you very much, and leave it at that.

It had been a girl that had got him started in the first place, back at uni. Art student, she'd been. What did he know about art? Fuck all, that's what. He'd been studying accountancy. But he was dying to get into her pants so he'd just gone and ripped a few things off, hadn't he? Triumph through adversity, all that. Of course, art had reached the stage where you could just chuck paint at a page, so that's exactly what he'd done. It was like the guy who'd done all the Stone Roses albums – John Pollock. He'd given it a bit of that, just made sure it looked a bit different. Disguised his influences.

> *udied accounting and finance at the University of East Anglia, but it was while he was an undergraduate there that he discovered his true passion for art. Encouraged by his girlfriend, an art student, and her tutors, Labourn laid down the foundations of his bleak, destructive visual manifesto. His work was well received in critical circles and he dropped out of his course to develop his craft and strengthen his artistic voice. Over the next ten years Labourn enjoyed a meteoric rise to the uppermost circles of the art world, and b*

'I love this one,' Jamey said, pausing in front of one canvas. It was six feet by nine and, true to the young journalist's word, a visceral nebula of red laced with currents of black. He'd chopped up a newspaper page and rearranged the amputated sentences and paragraphs across the painting. Behind it all loomed the twin monoliths of a stencilled number eleven.

'This one really sums up where I am right now, artistically,' Labourn said automatically. He kept to the script when discussing his work, just in case.

'It's really profound,' she said, and turned to him, 'Do you know how much your work has influenced me? I've changed my whole lifestyle, everything. I dropped out of university, moved away from home. I met up with others who were followers of your message.'

He nodded. It was a familiar story. He had some full on fanatics out there. They did all sorts of weird shit when they got together. He'd been to a couple of their gatherings, mainly on the pull, of course. Mad stuff. He had no idea what they saw in his stuff – certainly nothing he'd put in there. Amazing what people found in shit on a page.

'What makes this piece stand out for you?' he asked, genuine for the first time that day.

'It's so profound,' she said again, eyes glazing slightly, 'The textual dissemination really speaks clearly to me. And the numerical motif, it's just incredible. I love it.'

Numerical motif? She meant the eleven. He always put an eleven in there somewhere, but this time he'd started with it, a big fuck-off eleven down on the sheet, first thing he'd done. He'd got a bit stuck with this one, artist's block or whatever. So he'd just put the eleven there first and gone over it later. What she thought it all meant he did not know. The eleven was just something he'd stolen from the KLF. They always had a hard on for twenty-three. Something about it being a special number, a prime number. Consecutive. They put it everywhere and people went mad for it, so he'd nicked the idea. Made it an eleven instead. Job's a good 'un.

She turned to him, shuffled her feet slightly.

'My friends and I, we...' she began.

'Yes?'

'Well, we know you often meet people outside of exhibits, and... you know.'

'Sure,' he said, smiling. Here we go.

'Well we have a meeting planned, tonight. I'd really like it if you could come. You understand, don't you?'

'Perfectly,' he purred, 'Don't you worry. Like I said, I'm always happy to please my fans. Just tell me the time and the place.'

'Oh, it's here,' she said.

'Here?' he said in surprise.

'We've booked a function room at the gallery. If you can be here just after eleven...'

'Huh.' He thought. 'I'm guessing they've no idea what you've got planned?'

'Oh no,' she smiled, 'Of course not.'

'How many of you are going to be there?'

'Ten,' she said promptly.

He nodded, 'Ten. Good number. Well I'll definitely be there. No problem.'

'Great,' she said, smiling brightly, 'We knew you would.'

'Well,' he said, looking at his watch, 'I'm sorry I can't complete the tour but I've got to be somewhere. I'll see you tonight though.'

'Yes. I can't wait,' she said, and practically skipped away without a further word, leaving Labourn stood before his canvas.

He looked at it, wondering again what they all saw in there. It really was just a load of crap. Why would she think this one stood out from any of the others he'd slapped together up and down this hall? A bigger fucking eleven than usual? What else had she said? Something about textual insemination?

> *His use and rearrangement of written texts was regarded by critics as a sustained assault on the written word and his canon as a whole is commonly regarded as a ferocious critique of the cult of meaning. Unlike*

He leaned forward to make out the clippings he'd used. He usually forgot what he'd used as soon as he'd finished slicing it up – what the page had to say didn't matter much to him. As long as you kept it a bit general you could get mileage out of any old subject. Cheers for that one, Picasso. What was that painting called? *The Guitar and the Journal.* Something like that. He remembered going into the uni library and thumbing through a few books on art looking for stuff to nick and that one had stood out for some reason.

He squinted. This one looked like a biography of someone, out of a newspaper. He couldn't remember where he'd got it from, or why it had been in there. Definitely a newspaper.

He leaned back again. Shouldn't be seen staring at his own work as if he'd never laid eyes on it before. Never knew who was watching. Anyway, what did it matter what the silly bitch thought? She had a tight arse, and that was enough for him. And now he had himself a little 'gathering' to attend. Sorted. They may be a daft bunch of twats but they had some good fucking fun when they wanted to. Ten of them too, that was a new record. And to think they were gonna do it here. Mark bloody Peterson would have a right old rush of blood to the head if he knew about that. Mind, he'd probably approve of how bloody pretentious they'd manage to make it, if it was anything like the last couple he'd been to.

He looked at his watch again. Twenty past three. He had to go. Better stop off at a chemist on the way if he wanted to dress for the occasion.

> *destruction of the sign was deeply negative. His rending of coherent texts and their seemingly random scattering across turbulent, abstract vistas implied both the failure of the sign and a fractal element of larger cha*

The darkness was clasped in a thin sheet of fog as Labourn pulled up in the gallery's car park. Through it he could see lights on in one of the function rooms. He checked himself in the mirror and stepped out. The night air carried a shoal of tiny needles across his cheeks and down the back of his neck.

He breathed out, eyes darting warily across the car park. Satisfied, he went over to the main entrance. The doors were unlocked and there was no one at the desk. He looked around, and saw most of the doors were locked, lights off behind them. Then he saw a piece of paper on the counter, picked it up.

Room 10B, East Wing.

He looked. The lights were on and the door yielded under his push. He went through. Strange that there was no guard about. Very trusting of the gallery. He wondered how they'd manage to arrange something like this. He probably had a fan working here, pulling a few strings. Besides, all he'd done with this gallery he probably had the freedom of the city of modern art. As long as his exhibit was safely behind lock and key. Don't want some twat wandering in off the street and nabbing himself twenty mil of my bloody art. Although fair play to whoever was going to perambulate out the front door with a nine foot fucking canvas, eh?

He found 10B. It was the last room on the wing.

> Critical reception to Labourn's work was uni-
> formly divided throughout his life and will
> doubtless continue to be so for years to come.
> Supporters of his work were numerous and fanati-
> cal – no other artist in living memory inspired
> such devout support amongst the art community.

They were stood in a circle. He counted, nine of them. A few lads, mostly girls. No complaints there. All twenty-something at best. Again. Still young enough to believe in something. There was Jamey, stood at the front of them.

All the furniture had been pushed to the edge of the room bar the one table they were congregated around, placed exactly in the middle. He wondered what that was all about. There was something placed on the table, but he couldn't see past them to make out what.

'Hi,' he said pleasantly, 'Am I on time?'

Jamey looked at her watch, 'Yes, perfectly.'

That was a bit pedantic. It was only a joke, love. As if I care.

'It's a bit uncomfortable looking in here,' he said, looking around, 'I hope this isn't it.'

A smile shimmered across the group. He felt an itch at the back of his head. Something was up here.

'Well? What are we waiting for?' he demanded. None of them moved, just stared at him.

'Why, the time,' Jamey said in surprise.

'The time? What time?' he said. 'I didn't think this was a military operation.'

'Okay,' she said.

Stop bloody staring like that. He took a step back towards the door. This wasn't panning out how he expected, that much was bloody certain. Something was going on here.

> *The dissonance between signifier and signified in his work represents a destruction of meaning, of the sign itself. Labourn's art suggests entropy as the ultimate destination of reality.*

He felt the door open behind him. A very young looking security guard had stepped through, and was locking the door behind him.

'Hang on,' Labourn said, 'Can someone tell me what the fuck is going on here?'

They stepped forward collectively. He caught a glimpse of gleaming metal beneath the strip lights. What the *fuck* was on that table?

'You know, Philip,' she said, 'We all know, don't worry. Everything has been building up towards this. Come on now.'

'I really don't know what you're fucking talking about, you know that?' he told her, 'Clearly there's been a breakdown of communication here, because this is *not* what I had in mind, I'll tell you that for fucking free.'

'Yes, exactly,' she nodded, 'A breakdown.'

They began to walk towards him, and he finally saw through their ranks to the table. There was a big roll of what looked like canvas laid across it, and next to that...

Oh fuck.

'Listen,' he said, holding his hands out, backing away 'I really don't know what you people have figured out with all your pretentious chin-stroking bullshit, but I'm really not into this fucking shit, okay? Okay? I just put any old crap down, you know? It's just a piss-take!'

'Yes,' one of the men said. He was taller than Labourn, looked strong, 'The futility of expression. We know. A spiral, a collapse into destruction. It's all perfectly clear, Philip.'

Jesus Christ. This is what they'd read into his shit? He was going to have to give it some gab and quickly or he'd be leaving in a fucking bucket, wouldn't he?

They closed in on him.

'*Listen*,' he blurted, 'You're wrong, you've got it wrong, okay? None of what you're saying is correct. You've read it all wrong. I'm sorry, but my work is just a load of shit smeared on a page. I never put any thought into it, I swear to fucking God, it's just a load of crap!'

They paused briefly, then Jamey nodded, turned to the others.

'This is expected,' she said, 'As the totality reaches its final collapse it will go through a phase of self-destruction. Do you remember *Composition 7*? The system violently inverts itself.'

What? *Composition 7* was one of his pieces. His eyes widened. There was no blagging this one. They weren't taking no for an answer. Whatever they thought he'd been telling them, it was set too deeply in stone to be erased now.

He sprung forward suddenly, heading for a window, but his feet went from under him before he took one pace and he went sprawling to the carpet. He turned and saw the security guard standing over him. The others closed around him as he tried to scramble to his feet. His mind finally went blank as they lifted him forcefully towards the table.

> *ay in tragic and unpleasant circumstances on*
> *Friday, 11th November, aged 30. The artist was*

'For fuck's sake,' he choked, 'Why?'

> *blic statement was issued the next day by a group*
> *claiming to be implicated. The message claimed*
> *to have been written by a group of his dedicated*
> *followers, and made the disturbing claim that*
> *Labourn's murder was 'The ultimate conclusion of*
> *his work and vision' Police investigation is*

Jamey looked down at him sympathetically, 'Even you can't tell us that, Philip.'

My Hard Luck

JO ELSE

✓✓✓

Nice writing

AGAIN TODAY. BEFORE 8.30am. Before I had even had a chance to have breakfast. Her knees in the small of my back. From my shoulder blades down to my coccyx I now have a mass of bruises at different stages of healing and different colours: red, soft blue, hedge green and the purple of a thundercloud. When I turn my back to look at them in the bathroom mirror they're really rather beautiful, a painter's palette of skin haemorrhages. I look at my face in the mirror, above these colours, gaunt, my eyes bloodshot, hair greying and straggly. My body is very thin, ribs sticking out in places. I have given up proper meals, tending to subsist on coffee and croissants during the day as I don't want to spend any length of time in the kitchen when she might walk in. We haven't eaten or cooked together since Christmas, when we'd both kept to our bedrooms and our separate televisions and laptops. The radiators had stopped working in the bitter cold and we'd been wrapping ourselves up in our coats. Before that her expertise never went much beyond an aubergine casserole which she'd usually burn. Odd how burnt food makes such an insult, burnt aubergines a double insult.

I gaze at my appearance. I could almost be a depiction of suffering by a great master. Perhaps Caravaggio without the arrows. I did an art history course when I was at college and I always rated him. A kind of punk renaissance man: women, men, boys, girls, fights, booze, fast horses and art. But really I'm very low brow. I watch reality television and soaps and though I went to university twenty years ago it isn't so you'd notice. I work in a library but I haven't actually opened a book in ten years to read. I love movies though: film noir, Almodovar, Russian shorts, X-Men, anything. I put on a movie like some people reach for a drink. I'm lowbrow but Karen is beyond low brow. She fills in puzzle books, watches Ant and Dec, Westlife Christmas specials and Harry Hill's TV burp. She's worked in a clothes factory in Tottenham since she was 18. She has no interests other than food, TV and social networking sites. Just a handful of friends, all as bovine as her. She is uninterested and uninvolved and unintelligent. She was amazed to hear that asbestos was dangerous, for example. And she is completely unloved by me. Strike that, utterly unloved by me. And she knows it. I am still uncertain why I married her. I was 35, worried about being alone. She was slimmer then, prettier, came when I came, laughed at the things I told her. Everyone told me she'd do; I told myself she'd do.

I think Marco at work is becoming aware of how things are. Marco, 25-ish, always comes to work in neat black jeans and a green T-shirt. Small moustache, impossibly neat. Maybe gay but perhaps not willing to commit either way just yet. Resisting the gays with their megaphones on one side and the straights on the other, all willing him to choose. Because you must choose, they always want you to choose. But I hope he sits on the fence as long as he likes and kicks out at the whole lot of them.

I perch on the chair at the computer, inputting a new load of books onto our system, every now and then wincing as I move. Marco has been watching, constantly about to open his mouth, but then stopping himself and getting me coffees from Monty's instead. I've had three since I got in and now it's only 11am. At this rate, I'll be totally wired by noon. Marco is a good man but he doesn't know how little he can help me. I'm in this with her, like Fred McMurray and Barbara Stanwyck in Double Indemnity. Right down to the end of the line. Whatever happens, we signed up for it.

I suppose it was my own fault I got clobbered. She bought a new dress at the weekend, for work, it was a size 14 but she couldn't get into it. I watched her this morning from the kitchen whilst she tried it on in the lounge. She strived and strived and strived and then she burst out crying, throwing it aside, standing there wobbling in her pants. She must be 16 stone at least by now. She saw me looking at her and went for me, though I didn't say a word, she still went for me. Perhaps if I had gone up to her, put my arms around her, comforted her, she wouldn't have hit me. Perhaps we would have been able to carry out restoration work on the sick property that is our marriage. But I've long been unwilling to put my arms around that girth. I wish she didn't make me sick but she does. A year ago, when she first complained of putting on weight, I bought her a gym membership. She went a few times only, always stopping off at the chip shop on her way back. That's how she is, a walking defeat of a person.

It's 1pm. The library is getting quiet, just a few old people and some mums and kids. And of course the smellies, the stinking homeless or the unemployed who come in for warmth and quiet and maybe the chance of a quick kip. There have been many corporate initiatives over the years to get rid of them but I believe the smellies should always have a place to go. In the cold unfriendly 21st century they need the quiet of a library more than ever. We're supposed to throw them out but I never do. And don't get me started on the idea of libraries with coffee bars and music and noise, as though we were an American chain of coffee shops. I will torch this library before I let that happen to this place.

Marco interrupts my chain of thought with a sound that is closer to a whisper than a voice.

'Paul, you have to talk to me. Tell me what's going on.'

'There's nothing going on,' I reply.

'Since Christmas, coming in looking like death. Almost falling asleep at the desk and you don't even have kids, the way your back always seems to hurt you. What's happening?'

'Really nothing, just some injuries from sport and...'

'You don't play sport!'

'Squash, yes, I absolutely play squash. Look, there are maybe a few marital issues but nothing I can't handle.'

I laugh at the phrase marital issues, it's somehow totally inaccurate though it sounds civilised enough. Marital issues, there are no marital issues. I just can't stand the fucking sight of her.

Marco sighs.

'Take some time off, speak to Jake. Please. You look exhausted.' Jake is our roving library manager. Moving, or roving, between us and the large library at Camden.

There's a small queue of people now waiting at the counter to check out books and DVDs. Marco reluctantly leaves me and heads towards them. I ponder his words and go outside for a quick fag. A rainy chilly cold day in May – the predicted heat wave has as usual failed to materialise. I think it will be like this forever in Britain now. Summers that permanently resemble autumn. I return inside and the afternoon drifts away. I do some more inputting, stack some books, help a young boy find a DVD he really wants, text a friend. I keep busy, it's coming up to five.

She gets in at five from her job. One of the things I loathe so much about her is that she is a terrible creature of habit. She never goes shopping before coming home, or for a coffee or tea. Or even a drink. She always comes straight back, puts on the kettle and lays her cup at precisely the same place on the kitchen surface, a large blue one with red roses on it. The sort an old lady in a nursing home might cherish. Whenever I see it I want to break it. She gets into a terrible rage if anyone else uses it by mistake. Usually by the time I get home at seven it's stacked away but once she'd left it on the draining board and I picked it up for one minute by its handle. Thinking. Just thinking. I decide to go for a drink and put off going home until around eight. I go alone to The Bear which is just 200 yards from the library. I ask Marco but he's busy tonight. She hates it when I go out after work. She feels I should be home at the same time as her and even though we have barely talked for months, I get a text asking when I'm coming home. I don't answer it.

8pm, I put the key in the lock, she's sitting in the darkened lounge watching TV. She swivels her eyes round to me, like the head movement of some strange prone monster. She says nothing and turns back to the TV. I go to the kitchen for a cup of water. I see that her cup is stacked rather precariously over the top of the draining board. As I fill my own cup with water my jacket accidentally brushes against her cup, and in ten seconds it's on the floor in pieces. I hear her go alert in the sitting room. Within seconds she's in the kitchen, white with fury.

'Karen, it really wasn't my fault, it was the way it was perched on the draining board. I'm sorry, I...' I really try hard to placate her. I am actually really sorry to have broken it. I know it means a lot to her.

'You,' she splutters incoherently, a great blubbering incoherent mess, 'You' again through her sobs, 'You just don't... you just don't care, do you?'

And the thing in me is torn and the beast is let out.

'You got that one right didn't you?' I scream back at her and I tell her I am out of here tonight, 'Keep the house, keep the money. I am gone.'

Though as I say that I wonder where exactly I will be going – my parents? They don't really like me, they feel bad about it but they prefer my sister. She is genuinely kind. I just fake kindness when I feel like it or when it's useful to me. I can love films and animals but I struggle with people, except in the general sense, like at the library. I can chat to a lonely old woman for hours. I am good with strangers, I make them feel liked and cared for. I remember, as Karen stands there crying fatly, how I burned my sister's plait with a Bunsen burner when we were at school together. We are twins born ten minutes apart. She wouldn't speak to me for weeks. So, it doesn't look like I'll be going there either, and my friends, well they like me and I amuse them but they don't associate me with need. I would be embarrassed for them to associate me with need. Really I would.

I notice that Karen has gone very quiet, a yellow black light coming out of her eyes. Almost as though she is on drugs. She has one hand behind her back. I wasn't really concentrating while I ranted my piece to her but I think I know what she holds behind her back. And then it starts. It starts raining down.

On my arms, my shoulders, finally my stomach, near to and soon into the artery at the top of my legs, the one that will kill you if it starts to bleed.

And God how it does bleed. She doesn't stop, she just keeps going, again and again with the blade and I am trying to defend myself with my hands over my head and they're getting slashed and bloody and I'm on the floor. Beginning to feel distant, foggy, my head contracting and expanding. I can see from a long way down how the police will find her and me, my funeral, at some leafy cemetery or graveyard, my mother both laughing and crying with her strange version of happy grief. My father so tight-lipped it's impossible to tell whether he is upset or not. He's possibly relieved and dare not admit it. My sister cold, remembering the Bunsen burner, Marco probably the most upset because he could not save me, white and pale in his green T-shirt and combats. Jake, glancing at his mobile from time to time, aware he has a meeting ahead but not wishing to show a lack of compassion for the family of a 'valued employee'.

Well, at least I've been that. Maybe they should put it on the plaque they get for me at the cemetery. Not a loving husband, a good son or a kind brother or a particularly reliable friend but a valued employee. And really, when we don't love people, when we no longer attempt to love people, when we can no longer bear people and yet we cannot be compassionate, then we deserve everything we get. My misfortune that I am dying here in this kitchen, with blows and blood and damnation rained down upon me from my uncared for, wretched wife. My hard luck.

Backwards

MELVIN BURGESS

Good writing but the end is odd

A MURDER WAS committed in the park in front of
Owen Davies' house one Friday night. A young
woman aged 24, wearing a short black coat and knee
boots, was assaulted and strangled on the muddy grass
shortly after midnight, while Owen slept. He found out
about it on Saturday morning, when a neighbour paused
and told him the news.

'Just over there.' The neighbour nodded to an array
of police tape and uniforms. It was official; an unofficial
death.

Owen stood and looked across the grass. A life cut
short, so near. It was the closest he had ever come to
murder.

He left for his workout at the gym. All day, the fact
of the murder rose up and down in his mind, like a
drowned body, he thought, rising and falling in the innocent water.

Over the weekend, more pieces of information
emerged. The girl's name was Rose. She was short, mixed
race, pretty. She had recently split up with her boyfriend.
She had been assaulted, but not raped. Then she had
been strangled with her own tights. There was no sign

89

of any struggle. Owen wondered, 'How do they know it was assault, then?' Perhaps she had known her assailant.

That night Owen looked from his bedroom window over the park, and marvelled at the magic of an ended life. Death. Past, present and future, all gone. Memories vanished as if they had never been. Feelings never felt, thoughts never known. Even the memory of memory had been extinguished in this young woman.

On Monday morning he began to collect information about the murder. The girl was single. Her name was Rose Elliott. She was popular, middle class, and well educated. Not your usual victim, he thought, but then, what did he know about murder victims?

She had studied forensic science at university. She wanted to be a police woman, but had been unable to find a job so far. The papers found that oddly exciting. She had worked part time in a bakery quite near the park. Owen found that oddly exciting. He used that bakery from time to time. Perhaps he had seen her, spoken to her. He might even have bought something from her. Perhaps.

That lunch time, he went to buy his lunch at the bakery where Rose had worked. He felt it was important that he had some contact with the dead girl.

The management had put a photo of her on the counter, with a box for contributions for flowers for her funeral. Owen bought a pasty and left five pounds.

That night, he wept for her. Even as his tears fell, he knew that the thought of her in death made her far, far more beautiful than she had ever been in life.

The next day, he continued finding out about Rose. He told himself that finding out about her was now her only memory – a form of substitute life for the dead girl.

He learned the name of her family, her friends. He joined the Facebook group in her remembrance. Finally, he scanned a newspaper photograph of her into his computer and sat, sipping wine, watching her face for signs of movement. Of course there were none.

On a website that evening, he had a bit of coup. He discovered her address from a careless remark.

Late at night, he went to visit Rose at her home. He waited outside, peered in through the windows. He felt that by behaving as if she was alive, he was giving her a form of life. He didn't call her name, though – he wasn't that stupid. He left when someone came out of the house and called to him. A woman. In bed at home, he dreamed that it was really Rose.

The next day he bought his lunch at Rose's bakery again. When he got home in the evening, the police announced that they were looking for a man. Rose, it seemed, had been stalked. A man had been seen hanging around outside her house and place of work in the days leading up to the murder. There were several witnesses. The police had a detailed description. He had been wearing a dark green walking jacket, a black woolly hat with the word 'Thinsulate', written on a white label on the front. He had worn jeans and trainers. A wisp of blonde hair straggled out from under his hat.

Owen went to bed that night in a state of great excitement.

The next day, a Wednesday, he took the morning off work and went into town. He bought himself the murderer's outfit: the black hat, the jeans, the trainers. It was all easy to find. Only his hair was incorrect – his was too dark. He solved this by buying himself a wig. The photo-kit looked so like him, his heart sang.

He spent the night sitting at home in full attire, talking to Rose on the PC. It felt so good.

The next morning, he again took time off work to keep track of developments in the investigation on the news. He only ventured out once, to buy a local paper at midday.

To be turning into someone else – to be turning into a man who stopped lives. It was just so right.

He fell asleep on the sofa, and when he woke up the next day, it was already Friday. He couldn't believe it. He had missed a day – but where? He had no memory of the missing hours. Time seemed to have jumped forward.

He spent the day at home, sweating, biting his nails, overcome with the feeling that his pleasant dream was about to turn into a nightmare. He spent the time searching for stories about himself in the local and national newspapers. Had this happened before? His sense of identity was slipping along with time. He was not himself.

It was almost midnight when finally he got the courage to take some air in the park. He strayed off the grass to play it safe. A mistake.

It was not until he saw the girl come towards him, smiling, holding out her tights in her hand, that he realised. He had not jumped forward a day at all. He had jumped back a week.

The Double Devil

MELVIN BURGESS

Brill!

A YOUNG GIRL sits looking out of her window. She doesn't like what she sees. She doesn't like much. She doesn't like her parents, she doesn't like her school. She doesn't like the dirty, run down Burnley estate outside the window pane.

'If I could be fabulously rich,' she sighed. 'If I could have that, I would give anything.'

A ring at the door. She runs down and opens it. A young man stands there. He smiles.

'I,' he says, 'Have come to make your dreams come true.'

Years pass. The girl, in her late teens now, is sitting in her room looking out of a different window. The view across LA is splendid. It is one of many such appartments in many splendid towns that she now owns.

There is a noise behind her. She looks up. There stands the young man.

'So soon?' she asks. 'You haven't aged at all.'

'You have,' says the young man. He laughs. He takes two steps forward. He seizes her by the neck.

'I own your soul,' he hisses. He reaches inside – and groans. Calmly, the girl removes his hand from her throat.

'Did you imagine,' she says, 'that the King of Heaven in all his Majesty could create nothing worse than you?'

The young man groans and takes a step back.

'Who are you?' he hisses.

'I alone, in all creation,' says the girl proudly, 'have nothing to fear from you. I alone have nothing to lose. I alone have been created in the true image of the living God. I alone, have no soul.'

The young man turns to run. But he can never run fast enough.

The Copie I met in the taxi in Leicester

Our Candyfloss Beach

ROSIE JONES

This is a great example of shite. Shite shite !!!

L ET'S GO ON a trip to the seaside, you and me. You
will be tired from your long shifts at the hospital and
I will be reluctant to drive that far when the weather is
so unpredictable. But as soon as you walk in the door,
your tiredness collapsing in my arms, I shall realise that
we must get away from our lives, if only for one day.

You will sleep for the majority of the monotonous
journey to the seaside. When I am stuck amongst a con-
coction of eager caravans and impatient sports cars, I look
over to you and smile. Even when your eyes are framed
by bags of insomnia, and your chin has been attacked by
spots of stress, you are beautiful. Every so often, gentle
sighs will escape from your slightly parted lips, making
me think back to the beginning of our relationship – do
you remember? We seemed to spend every moment of
every day kissing. When we'd pull away, my lips would
tingle slightly before we'd smile and lean in for one more
kiss. Kissing seems less of a priority now.

After four hours, we will arrive at the desolate seaside.
Apparently, nobody goes to the seaside in November.
Stretching away your tiredness, you will snap at me and

tell me to open the boot. Doing as I am told, you will pull out your thick red duffel coat, the one with big black buttons. Once we are wrapped up in coats, scarves and hats, I will interlock my fingers in yours and begin walking down to the promenade.

It won't be until we are further down that we realise that the sand is missing. Perhaps it has fallen in love and run away with the sky. As a replacement, bales of pink clouds line the beach, as if they are waiting to be collected by an old-fashioned farmer. We shall look each other in the eyes and smile as we realise what the pink clouds are: candyfloss.

With your petite hand firmly snuggled in mine, we will start to run down the promenade until we reach some stairs to take us down to the beach. Climbing onto a particularly large bale of candyfloss, you will tear off a thin strip and pop it in my mouth. The softness melts as soon as it touches my tongue. Instinctively, we will both lie on the pink mattress and stare into each other's eyes. We always laughed at the fact that we could have a whole conversation without uttering a single word, but it was true. Your slow and heavy blinks will tell me that you are tired. Not just because of work, tired of us. Where were the wasted days of sleep? What had happened to your carefree attitude? When had your work become bigger than our relationship?

After an immeasurable amount of time, you will pull my hand into consciousness and drag me into the distance with you. The beach seems to yawn for miles and miles. We will try to count the bales of candyfloss as we walk but will lose count and interest. We will stop and listen as we faintly hear music coming from the speakers in the sky. The music will be turned up until we smile in acknowledgement. Michael Buble. Your favourite singer. Do you remember when we first moved in together? After a hard day's work, you would put your Michael Buble CD on and beg me to dance with you. I would always say I was too busy with work or cooking dinner. But looking at you, all I will want to do is dance. I will take hold of your slender waist and you will rest your head on my shoulder, allowing your soft brown curls to trail down my back. We will sway to the music until the sky runs out of songs.

I will then notice a small cottage a few metres from where we were dancing. Walking arm in arm up to the cottage on the water's edge, we will realise that the cottage's walls are made out of marshmallows, piled on top of each other. Your constant craving for marshmallows will give in as you reach for a handful and gobble them up. We will then notice a plant pot at the doorway of the cottage, overflowing with melted chocolate. Simultaneously, we will grab even more marshmallows and dip them in the chocolate. We will then let the chocolate dribble down our throats, warming our insides. You will laugh at a drip of chocolate that escapes my mouth and runs down my chin. Touching my face with your chilled gloveless hand, you will reach up and gently kiss away my chocolate stain.

Creaking the door open just wide enough to peep inside the cottage, we will succumb to curiosity and sneak through the marshmallow entrance. The oak floorboards will ache and moan as we walk towards the table, piled high with photo albums, at the centre of the otherwise empty room. As we take an album each, we will gasp as we see whose memories these photo albums hold: ours. We will laugh at our haircuts and sense of fashion when we first met each other. We were so young weren't we? As we flick through the pages, we will feel ourselves flicking through our years together, watching each other change from a pair of lovesick teenagers into an embracing married couple with evident laughter lines. Our smiles will disappear as we reach the final photograph in the final photo album. It will be a captured memory of the three of us, you, me and him. We are smiling. We will wonder how could someone that gave us so much joy in the past give us so much pain in the present.

Needing to move on from the final haunting photograph, I will then follow you out of the cottage, stopping at the water's edge. Once we are there, you will slowly unbutton those big black buttons on your thick, red duffel coat, slip it off and lay it on a nearby bundle of candy floss. Without you telling me to do so, I will gentle remove your black chiffon dress to reveal your red lace bra with matching knickers. Once I am undressed, I shall touch the tips of your fingers and lead you into the water until it is lapping against your shoulders. The sea shall be as warm and as bubbly as that bath I made you six months ago. Every so often, we will point and laugh when we see a rubber duck passing by. Kissing your shoulder, you will gently sigh as I remove your bra, and let it float off towards the pink horizon. Wrapping your perfectly slender legs around my waist, our lips will finally find each other.

It will then start to rain. The cold droplets on our cheeks strikingly contrast with our close warm bodies. Simultaneously, we will both tip our heads towards the sky and open our mouths. The lemony tang will fizzle on my tongue as I realise that it is raining homemade lemonade. When our thirst has been quenched, we shall run back to our car to avoid the sugary, sticky rain.

On the way home, we will laugh about the day. You will then apologise for being so preoccupied with work. We will then talk about that day. The day you shrieked from his nursery. The day we desperately tried to blow our lives into our son's fragile mouth. The day we came home from the hospital, no longer a family.

When we arrive back home, you will lead me to the bedroom and kiss me passionately. As we make love for the first time in six months, I will feel as close to you as I did in the beginning, before we knew the meaning of heartbreak. Afterwards, you will face away from me, taking my hand and placing it on your stomach. I will feel you smile as I kiss your shoulder blade. After a while, you will turn to me and whisper what I had been stopping myself from saying all day out of fear of being answered with a cold silence: 'I never stopped loving you.' And we will start again, on our own candyfloss beach.

Elvis and the Neighbours

LOUIS MALLOY

M Y MOTHER COULDN'T make up her mind whether she liked having Elvis as a neighbour or not. Whenever we heard the first strummed guitar chord, she would sigh as if her whole evening was about to be ruined. But she still listened and even turned the radio off sometimes while she sewed or ironed. Then he'd do one of those weird bits of singing like we'd never heard before. A grunt or a wail or a 'hey, baby' and my mother would turn to my father and ask why anyone would sing like that when they actually had quite a nice voice. Dad just read his book and I said I liked how Elvis sang. It was different. It was fun.

The house next door had been empty for a long while before Elvis moved in. He had come over for a few months to visit his great-aunt, who was in an old people's home somewhere. It didn't seem much of a way to spend a holiday, but he always looked happy and his manners were impeccable. That was what got my mother's approval, in spite of the singing. He called her 'ma'am' and my dad 'sir'.

Everyone was curious because he looked so different. On a dull rainy evening in Lady Bay he'd walk down the road like a sudden burst of show business. Tight jeans, pink jacket and his hair greased up into jet black sweeps and swirls. And blue suede shoes.

'Blue suede,' said my mother, a dozen times to her friends. 'Suede. In blue. I mean for a bag maybe. But shoes. Shoes!'

He didn't seem to go out for any purpose, never carrying a shopping bag or even a chip supper. You'd just see him walking in that easy rolling way, with the grin and the dark, faraway eyes.

One Sunday afternoon he put a chair by his front door and started playing guitar and singing outside. People going by slowed down and most of them smiled at him and nodded, but no one dared to stop. He sang in that strange way and my mother kept up the usual commentary.

'That's an opera song. "O Sole Mio". It's not called "It's Now Or Never" at all.' But still she listened and didn't put the radio on till he'd finished.

Elvis left in December. He came round to say goodbye and my mother insisted on giving him some apples and chocolate for the journey. My father and I walked down to the stop and waved him off. He saluted us from inside the bus and winked, then disappeared towards town, towards the world.

When we got back home my mother was doing no sewing or ironing, just sitting and listening to the silence. She was still looking at the corner of the room where Elvis had been standing ten minutes earlier and where she would one day keep her boxes, filled with every record he ever made.

Home

MASON HENRY SUMMERS

I WAKE UP early to find I'm a semi-detached council house in Surrey. Living room, kitchen with dining room attachment, three bedrooms and two bathrooms. Built circa 1954 in the post-war housing boom. Four children run around me, making a lot of noise, so I decide to go back to sleep. Two hours later I'm awake again as a swimming pool in a California ranch house, up on the ridge overlooking Hollywood. The owner, an ageing movie star, takes a few laps in me but he's getting on now and spends more time lying on a lounger next to me, reading a Herman Wouk novel, waiting for his grandchildren to come visit.

I wake at midday and I am a public school in the south of England, late in its day, its glory waning. Cold fills my long, empty corridors and the smell of old churches fills the classrooms. In one of my bathrooms children weep, again and again over the decades, frightened and alone, on the cusp of forcing their feelings back down inside themselves where they will remain trapped for the rest of their lives. Arrogance and fear float through me and as a whole I feel a lost, lonely ache. Once again I sleep.

Briefly I am a Victorian tower, a folly to celebrate a life long vanished from the world. I stand exposed and proud, immovable in the freezing winds that blast me through most of the year. My stone is dense and grey and inside I am dark and wet, a place of shadows and dirt, abandoned trinkets and human waste. Even through the thick stone I can feel a million tiny legs walking over me as swarms of ants move over me. I am just an obstacle for them, just another thing in their path.

By mid-afternoon I am one of those unusual glass walled houses that architects build for themselves to prove how smart they are. The sun bakes me, filling the solar panels on my west roof with warm, giving energy which I channel down to the underfloor heating in the lounge and study. The rest of the heat is absorbed into thick layers of warm, heavy insulation in my wall and roof cavities, hugging comfort in on myself. The architect's lonely wife pads over my toasty wooden floors while he's away on business and masturbates quietly in the study using one of his paperweights to pleasure herself. Her orgasm is very much like the sunshine when it comes.

Quickly now I am a flash of different places. I am a worn, old tent in a field in New England, I am a log cabin 35 miles outside of Juneau, I am a sun baked hovel in Egypt, a shelter made of branches and leaves somewhere in South America, too fast to tell where. Late afternoon and I am the remains of a Roman villa somewhere in Greece, half buried, forgotten, haunted by vague memories of languages no one ever speaks in me anymore.

I'm a children's hospital in Fallujah next, weary under the weight of human tissue and hurt. My walls are shot full of holes, my walls are soaked with blood and sorrow. I quickly go back to sleep. Awaking again I am a bicycle shed in a factory yard in a small Russian town, my thin walls chill and strong, alive with some small form of life I can't quite identify, some hardy fungus or spore that clings to me despite the awful shade of brown I have been painted. My wood inhales bitter smoke as a cyclist savours his last cigarette before the ride home.

The next time I am aware I can feel wood-chip wallpaper being coated with soft emulsion, careful long brush strokes against me. My walls are lined and lined with seventy years of wallpaper, never stripped off before the next application and the suffocating papery warmth jars against the tender decoration being done to me now. I have been bought by a young woman who has worked hard to have her own home and now she carefully gouges new holes in me for central heating and shelving and I can feel the cold dirt of a garden against the damp walls of a cellar which she doesn't know exists, as the doorway has been covered up years ago.

Now I am an art gallery somewhere near Houston, Texas. I am closed for the night and the only activity is the occasional sweep of a torch beam across the massive canvasses that hang on my walls as the guard makes his rounds. I can feel the soft, warm of the night and its noises pressing against me, lush vegetation hiding me from the world.

Last thing at night I am a tree-house, a unique and intricate design in a massive old oak at the edge of a country estate house. Bright moonlight soaks the tree and the branches which hold me up and together glow and vibrate with a simple joy. A rope ladder hangs like a dead weight from me, from the gaping hole in my main room's floor. My wood has been scarred and scratched by children and adults alike, each carving their own piece of their lives into me and each scar is a deep love bite in my happy form. Maybe one day they will return to see the lasting mark they have left in me and feel the distance between themselves now and themselves then and the aching nostalgia for another time. I go to sleep for the final time.

Sabotaging Bobby

DAN MALACH

T HREE MONTHS AFTER Dad's funeral Bobby calls me
and says come round. I *umm* and *ahhh*, but he says
it's important so I say okay. I go to his flat after work. As
soon as he opens the door I'm stunned – not only has
he shed something like three stone but also shaved off
that sorry horseshoe-of- denial hairstyle that really only
accentuated his pattern baldness. Following him through
the flat into the kitchen, my astonishment only grows.
For one, it's clean. Not show home clean, but at least
you don't walk down the hallway waiting for an oxygen
mask to drop. The kitchen's the same – gone is the leaning tower of crusted plates, the colony of flies swarming
around the bin. I take a seat at the table, upon which
there just happens to be a selection of dumbbells, while
Bobby puts on a black beanie that only comes three-quar-
ter ways down his forehead and brings out a whiteboard.
He leans it on the wall by the sink. Marker pen lofted like
a conductor's baton, Bobby tells me he has come up with
a plan. We stake out Oggy, get to know his routine – he
scrawls 'routine' on the whiteboard in blue letters – and
as soon as we know when he'll be alone we get a gun.

'Hold up a second,' I say. 'A gun?'

'You're damn right,' says Bobby.

'Okay Capone, where are you planning to get a gun from?'

Bobby gets his peeved face on. It's a face I know well and have seen many times before: the day he received a letter from university saying he'd failed his degree, the day he received a letter from Ruth – his only serious girlfriend – saying she was leaving him for the good of her soul, the day he received a letter from the publishing company saying his poetry was lovely, but sorry, they don't represent people with special needs. It's no wonder Bobby has a pathological hatred of the postal service.

'I met this guy online,' says Bobby. 'I can get a gun.'

'Sure you can, Bobby. Just email the friendly online arms dealer.'

'I'm being serious!' I sigh and shake my head.

'That's the problem. I think you are.' Bobby pouts angrily.

'So, are you in?' I push my chair back, stand up and go to get my coat.

'Well?' asks Bobby.

'In what, exactly?'

'In with the plan!'

I tell him he's insane.

'I'll tell you what's insane,' he says. 'Some junky scumbag kills our father and is now a free man. *That's* insane.'

'That's not quite what happened. It was an accident.'

'Who's to say he won't do it again, huh? Kill someone else's father while he's high on drugs, huh?'

'He was clean, you moron. The police tested him. But why bother with facts when convenient bullshit will do?'

'Why are you defending him?'

Bobby works himself up into such a furore that his face is shiny with sweat. I put on my coat and suggest perhaps he needs a holiday, preferably somewhere with a padded cell.

'I'm not the one that needs a holiday,' he says. 'You need a holiday!' I start laughing, which is probably not a great idea. Jowls quivering, he points a finger at me and says, 'Each man is his own measure. Neither more nor less.'

I ask him which self-help book he spat that from.

'Let yourself out,' says Bobby, turning back to the whiteboard where he starts drawing various apparently random crosses and arrows, his back-fat jiggling under his T-shirt. I call from the doorway that maybe he should get himself a hat that actually covers his ridiculous melon head.

* * *

I'm not saying the last three months have been easy for me because they have not. Gone are the days when I surfed into Compel-Sysao on a wave of glory as Computer Weekly's Technical Architect of the Year. I built C-S such a robust infrastructure that they soon promoted me to Technical Director. Now I can barely direct my way out of the shower in the morning. What I'm saying is that Dad's death hit me pretty hard too. I always pictured him dying in hospital, after a noble fight against some noble disease, slipping from the world with me at his bedside, holding his hand, Bobby behind comforting Mum as Dad says some important last words to me like, 'You're head of the family now. I'm proud of you, son.' Conceited, I know, especially as Bobby is two years older – but no one in their right mind would want Bobby as head of their family. What I certainly didn't picture was Dad being crushed by the car of a reformed crack-head leaving his weekly therapy session.

Things are not much better at home where the marriage to my beautiful, considerate wife is in danger of being suffocated by her sympathy. Every time she speaks to or touches me it's accompanied by a sort of nervous/quizzical frown, as if she's concerned my superego is about to collapse into rubble now Dad's gone and she'll find me wiping my arse on the toilet wall instead of with paper. I stupidly make the mistake of telling Josie about what happened at Bobby's. She responds with a potted analysis of Bobby – in a bid to help me understand my grief she'd bought and digested a library of do-it-yourself psychology books – beginning with his lack of friends and social skills, continuing through his various failures in love and work and concluding with the statement: 'This is his way of making himself important in the family. He's making a play for your father's chair.'

'He can have it,' I say. 'I don't think a paisley La-Z-Boy will go with our leather suite.'

She doesn't laugh. When I try to kiss her in bed she gazes at me like I'm a puppy saved from the drowning sack. I lose my erection. She puts a hand to my cheek and tells me it's okay, we can just hug. For not the first time I go downstairs and tear into a bottle of whisky then pass out on the couch.

A month or so later it's Mum's birthday, so we go over to hers on Sunday for a party. By the time we arrive the place is teeming with uncles and aunts and cousins. I look around for Bobby, but can't see him. Just then the man placing fireworks in the back garden, dressed in military trousers and a tight black T-shirt that highlights tectonic plates of back muscle, who I thought to be Uncle Remmy

– he used to be a boxer and could hoist me up with one hand – turns around, and I see that it's Bobby.

'Wow,' says Josie. 'That is the most extreme transformation I have ever seen.'

His jaw is still a bit flabby, and there's gut action behind that super tight T-shirt, but the man-boobs have been honed into genuine pectorals. Gone too is the silly little hat, replaced now with a black beanie that fits. He comes over to greet us, and I make a family joke about Mum cooking enough salmon fishcakes for everyone. Bobby laughs in this odd gruff *hak-hak-hak* way, which is so very different from his usual high pitched like-me laugh, then flexes his biceps, Josie has a feel and says *ooooh*. Then he tells me to come to his car, an old, blue Ford. He bangs the glove compartment and it pops open. Inside is a gun. A real gun. It's black and old-looking, with a thin barrel and a trigger that shakes in its holding. It smells of grease. I weigh it in my palm. I realise that Bobby is actually and genuinely insane.

'Impressed?' he says.

I reply, 'So what we do is this. We take the gun apart, and bury all the pieces of it.'

He snatches it from my hand. 'What kind of man are you?'

'One who doesn't want to spend the next twenty years being sodomised in the shower.'

Just then Mum calls us from the doorway. Bobby slams the gun away and saunters back inside. Such is my sheer disbelief at this whole situation, it takes a few moments for my legs to catch up with my brain. By the time I get into the dining room Bobby has already taken Dad's old place at the head of the table. I say nothing. During lunch, Josie grips my hand. She whispers, 'Are you okay? With Bobby in your father's chair?' I tell her

I'm just fine. She gives me the kind of look you might give a man with no legs who has just told you he's going to be high jump champion of the world. 'I still think you're the best,' she says, glancing at Bobby with something that may or may not be a covetous glint in her eye.

'Thanks for clarifying that,' I reply, and pull my hand away.

All afternoon Bobby fields questions about what he's doing and compliments about how good he looks. He offers opinions on all manner of things, such as whether Cousin Ruth's attic is haunted.

'Who cares about ghosts these days when there are plenty enough scary things in the real world? Such as murderous junkies allowed to roam the streets.' Sage nods all round.

Or Cousin Maxi's dilemma over whether he should work night shifts, on which Bobby cogitates while bending an entire piece of beef with his fork before shoving the gravy-dripping lot into his mouth and saying, 'Your family comes first Maxi. Do what you need to for them. That's how my father lived and it's how I do too.'

Maxi strokes his stubbled chin and says, 'You're right, Bobby.'

And I start to think, what the hell is wrong with you people? Hello? This is Bobby you're listening to! Bobby who actually shat himself aged ten when faced with a popping jack-in-a-box from you, Uncle Maxi. Bobby who is unemployed now but whose last job entailed scraping foodstuffs from the inside of industrial vats. And then I think, you know what, to hell with you, Bobby. If you want to embarrass yourself pretending to be someone you're not then you can have your gun and spend the next ten years doing De Niro impressions in front of the mirror.

'Are you okay, sweetheart?' asks Josie.

'Oh, yes,' I say, 'Oh ho, yes-sir-eeee, yes.'

* * *

Some weeks later I'm at work staring at the wall when Bobby calls and tells me that tonight's the night. I ask what night. He says *the* night. I say, oh, well good luck with *that* then.

'Listen, Matt,' he says, 'I want you to come.'

'Why? To watch you blow your own balls off?'

'The place of one brother is by the side of the other.'

I hunch down and cup the phone with my hand.

'Are you out of your fat-headed brain? You're talking about killing a man! What happens if you get caught? What will it do to Mum if you go to prison?' Bobby says, 'No man is an island, entire of itself.'

I hiss into the handset, 'What the hell are you talking about? For god's sake cut the pseudo-guru bullshit and think for a minute what you're suggesting.'

'Join me.'

'Go to hell.'

'Join me.'

'In what? Casual murder?'

'In avenging our father.'

'Why should I?'

There's a moment's silence before he says, 'I've never said this before but I've always looked up to you and what you've achieved in life. I know with you there I will be strong enough to do this.'

I'm so gobsmacked that all I can do is make this nasal grunting sound, which he takes as an assent, and so tells me to be round to his for seven, sharp, before hanging up, leaving me with my phone in my hand, wanting to do something dramatic like smash it through the monitor, kick my desk over and scream, but in the end I do nothing. I just put the phone on my desk and stare at the wall again.

After calling Josie to tell her I'll be working late I head to Bobby's. On the way I practice snippets of the speech I'm going to give him: while I appreciate that you miss Dad, like we all do, and feel aggrieved about his death, like we all do, what you are planning to do is not what people in a civilized country, blah, blah, blah, but when I get to his the words evaporate. He greets me in a towel, his body slabbed with muscle, and for the first time in my life I feel inferior to him. The entire place is plastered with photographs of Oggy; leaving his block of flats, outside the bookies, buying fish and chips, his ratty little face captured in every conceivable expression. Dates and times and shorthand explanations line numerous whiteboards. Bobby opens a sports bag and shows me the gun, a pair of nunchucks, and a police-issue gendarme baton he bought from a tourist stall in Paris. I take out the nunchucks and ask him what he intends to do with these.

'These,' he says, taking them, 'are for any problems.' He swings and snaps them around his midriff and shoulders. 'Give me five minutes to throw some clothes on and we'll go.' He swaggers to the bedroom while I stand there fingering the recently grown roll of fat around my gut.

Bobby drives. I watch him from the corner of my eye. While I cut fingernail crescents into the flesh of my palm, he stares out at the road as if we're off to buy groceries.

'Are you sure you can hit him?' I ask.

'I can hit a squirrel between the eyes from twenty metres.'

I picture a stack of dead squirrels, their glazed dead eyes rolled upwards. My stomach shimmies up my throat.

'If we need to go in,' he says, 'then you take the baton.'

I try to imagine myself bludgeoning someone to death. I tell him that's hilarious. Bobby sighs and shakes his head.

'I'm glad you're not my son,' he says. That scoops me out. I face the window, seething.

We park in an alleyway near Oggy's flat and sneak around, hiding in some Specially Designated Bushes. The block is grotty, ex-council, unlit. Bobby pulls on a black balaclava that shows only his intense eyes and bulbous lips. I shudder, terrified of him for a second before I remind myself it's only Bobby. While he takes deep deliberate breaths, I hold down vomit. A car pulls up. The door opens and slams shut. Footsteps. Oggy comes into view. I had hoped seeing him would inspire something in me, hatred, blood-lust, something primeval and urgent, but I don't feel anything for him. I don't want to be here.

'You don't need me,' I whisper to Bobby and turn away.

'Don't you dare,' he hisses and grabs my shoulder. 'You *are* going to watch this.'

Bobby narrows his eyes at me, and I suddenly get it. I know why he wanted me to come with him. None of this has anything to do with Dad or revenge. I'm here to watch Bobby prove he's better than me.

Bobby sights the gun and puts his finger on the trigger and whispers, 'Come on... come on...'

A chance to be the bigger man, the better son, finally able to prove himself after 32 years of being the family joke while I cringe and moan beside him. Anger like I've never felt before surges through my body.

Bobby's finger tightens on the trigger.

'One... more... step...'

I dive on Bobby just as he fires. The bullet pings off stone. We roll around in the bushes. I hear Oggy running. I try to climb on top of Bobby, thinking I'm still stronger, but he flips me over. He jumps up and grabs the nun-chucks. His face is the black balaclava with blazing eyes and a teeth-drawn mouth. He flicks and spins the nun-chucks. I roll into a ball and clutch my face. The nun-chucks whistle by my ear. Then it stops. I stay curled up for a while. When I look, Bobby has gone. After a while I drag myself up and wipe the dirt off and get a taxi home.

Josie's waiting with her usual dose of overt sympathy, but for some reason it's not as annoying as before, and when habit drives me to the kitchen, to my crystal tumbler and dear Mr Glenfiddich, something stops me from pouring. I find myself putting the whisky away and joining Josie in the lounge. We sit together on the sofa. She puts her head on my lap. A second later we're ripping clothes off. At one point she starts to ask if I'm okay to do this, but she's quickly convinced. The next day at work things are also better. For some reason, it all seems a little *less* pointless than yesterday. Instead of going through the motions, I engage. I send an email to the General Director outlining an idea for a new development strategy, and I get one in return saying, 'Welcome back.'

Everyday, I go over that night, trying to work out why sabotaging Bobby's plan has seemed to kick-start my life again, but looking back I can't quite believe it was me drinking every night, me unable to perform in bed, me sitting at work on the verge of tears. I tell myself that it's because I stopped him killing an innocent man. I tell myself it's because I saved him from going to prison. I tell myself it doesn't matter anyway because I'm feeling much better now thank you very much. Selfish, I know, but for Bobby selfish has always been a lifestyle choice, so I guess this is his comeuppance. Maybe. I think about calling him, but it never seems to be the right time, although I know this translates to I don't want to find the time. Still, I get regular updates about him from Mum. He has a new job checking lids at a margarine factory.

A few months down the line though and it's his birthday, so I think enough is enough and decide to visit. We make arrangements by email. The tone of his mails can only be described as nonplussed. On the way I pick him up a new digital radio, something able to get stations from all round the world, because I remember he was into that a while back. The first thing I notice when he opens the door is that he's filled out again. The second thing is he's stopped shaving his head – it's furring out around the sides and back. We go through his flat and the place is a mess of strewn clothes, takeout food cartons, and dusty exercise equipment. The kitchen is a biohazard. But it's when I realise how *bare* it is now, all the photos of Oggy gone, all the whiteboards gone, that I get this crushing feeling inside. We sit at the table and I give him his present. He opens it and looks at the radio and does an 'oh yeah, that's a really good present' act, all raised eyebrows and nodding smiles, but I can see the weight of his life, of being Bobby, in his sad eyes and regular sighs. It's all too much. I start to apologise. Once I've started, I can't stop. I tell him I'm sorry for all the times I've mocked him, acted superior to him, not treated him with enough respect. I say that I should listen to him more because he's an interesting person and sometimes he has something interesting to say. I tell him how secretly jealous I was when he was in shape. Finally, I apologise for sabotaging

117

his plans of avenging Dad. Bobby smirks at me, but it's not a nasty smirk, more his old put upon look.

He says, 'You know something, Matt. Sometimes you can be a real dickhead.' I apologise for that too.

'I really do miss Dad,' he says. 'He always just... liked me.'

'I like you too,' I say. He gives a sharp-eyed look. I tell him to get up and I hold my arms out. As we're hugging he reaches around and pinches the flab around my waist that I've still not managed to shift.

'Don't worry,' he says. 'Happens to us all in the end.' He pushes me out and grins. 'At twenty he's slim, at thirty the gym, at forty may as well pack it all in.'

'Amen, Bobby. Amen.'

Chicken in a Cold Climate

SUZI LESTER

T HE DOORBELL HAD been ringing for a long time. Florence and I sat, eyes locked across the table, challenging each other. The room was dark, lit only by candles, and cold enough to turn your lips blue. We each wore several layers of clothing and were swathed in heavy blankets. On the table in front of us was a pot of green tea, two cups and a lemon drizzle cake. I picked up the sharp bread knife and held it up against the candle light, then pressed it delicately into the pale white icing. Florence coughed.

'Sore throat?' I enquired.

'The door?'

'I made the tea,' I said. 'And the cake.'

'I set the table.'

I shook my head and finished cutting the cake.

'Fine,' said Florence, standing up. 'But if I die of exposure you'll have only yourself to blame.'

'More cake for me then.'

Florence stomped off down the hall, muttering to herself. I felt the rush of icy air as she opened the front door and pulled my blanket tighter around me. As I sipped my tea I started to make a mental list of food and other things we needed. It was my turn to go shopping at the weekend. I was not looking forward to it. It was a two hour walk to the nearest shops and it was forecast to snow again. Still, I had to go up a hill so I could at least take the sled for the way back. It was our best find of the year – we found it lodged in a tree coming back from the cinema one day and immediately rescued it to take home. The cinema was on the mainland so we didn't manage to go very often but every month they had a special triple screening and we made the journey across. They were very random in their selections but the second film was nearly always *The Shining*. That particular day they had been showing it in between *Whatever Happened to Baby Jane?* and *Shirley Valentine,* which we've seen three times now. The first time we saw it, Florence spent the following week talking to the kitchen wall, while I gave monologues in front of the microwave. Then we saw *Withnail & I* and decided it might be a good idea to stop having chats with the kitchen and actually clean it.

Florence returned with her blanket bundled up in her arms. She had the same look on her face as when she has to do her taxes.

'What are you doing?' I asked, pouring some more tea. 'Who was it?'

'There was no one there,' said Florence. 'Just this.'

'What is it?'

'Lori, have you ever, um, wanted to get a pet?'

'A pet?'

'You see, when I went to answer the door just now, there was no one there. Well, there was *someone* there, but not a person.'

'What are you talking about, Flo? Have you got a baby in there or something? It's not Christmas.'

'A baby is a person, Lori. This is a chicken.'

'A chicken?'

She placed the blanket carefully on the floor and uncovered the creature. It stood there, bobbing its head uncertainly. I picked up my cup and moved to the other side of the room.

'What did you bring it inside for? Bloody hell, Flo.'

'I couldn't leave the poor thing out there on its own. It'd freeze to death. Anyway, maybe we'll get eggs?'

'That's a rooster, Flo.'

'Really? So no eggs then?'

'I wouldn't have thought so, no.'

'Oh. What a shame. What shall we do with it then?'

'How should I know? You found it, you tell me.'

'We could eat it, I suppose.'

'Florence! I'm a vegetarian, and even if I wasn't, there is absolutely no way I'd kill an animal with my bare hands.'

'You could bash its head in with a brick.'

'Florence!'

'Ok, ok. Sorry. Maybe we should take it to the mainland.'

'But it's Friday evening. We can't get off the island until Monday morning.'

'So we're stuck with a rooster for a couple of days. How bad can it be?'

'Fine. But you can look after it. I'm making some more tea.'

I walked backwards out of the room and went into the kitchen. While I was waiting for the kettle to boil I opened my laptop and logged onto the Internet. I typed 'rooster' into the search engine and a list of sites came up, most of them about the band Rooster. I clicked on a link to an ornithology site and scrolled down to a section about caring for chickens in winter.

'Yo, Flo?' I called. 'It says here that roosters are built for cold weather. He'll be fine outside. If we keep him cooped up, so to speak, he might turn on us.'

Florence appeared at the kitchen door looking doubtful. The rooster was standing beside her.

'That's as maybe. But he doesn't have any other chickens for company. Or anyone to feed him.'

'So we take him food. He can sleep in the garden.'

'A fox could get him.'

'When have you ever seen a fox round here?'

'I suppose...'

I folded my arms. 'Well then?'

'Ok, I'll take him out now. Come on Socrates, let's go outside.'

'Socrates?'

'Yeah. I thought he should have a name. Who do you think could have left him here? Do you think it could be some sort of clue?'

'Clue to what?'

'I don't know. Perhaps it's a code. Rooster could mean... well, something else. We have to figure out what it is and then that will lead us to the next clue.'

'Yes, all right Miss Marple. It just seems a bit unlikely. I've boiled the kettle, do you want some more tea?'

'Yes please. Come on Socrates.'

Florence was always looking for mysteries to solve. When we moved in the previous occupants had left a key in one of the bedrooms. Florence spent weeks trying to work out what it was for. She was convinced there was some old trunk or secret door hidden somewhere. There would be maps and treasure and letters, all left by some brilliant and mysterious character who had been forced to flee suddenly, but left this key behind in the hope that someone would find it and uncover his secret. It turned out to be a key for the old garden gate that had fallen off its hinges.

I was just refilling the teapot when Florence returned, Socrates still at her side.

'It's very odd,' she said. 'He won't go back out. He just keeps following me. Maybe there are foxes out there and we just don't know about them. They're cunning creatures, after all.'

'Where do you get your information on animals from, Roald Dahl?'

I got two dishes out of the cupboard, filled one with water and one with seeds, then put both on the floor. Florence and I sat huddled at the table, sipping our tea and wondering what to do. We'd never had anything to look after before, although we both loved animals. At least, we loved cats and dogs and other cute fluffy things. Roosters were a bit different. You can't cuddle a rooster. You could try, but it would probably have your eye out.

'I'll get some food for him tomorrow, when I go shopping. And I'll talk to that guy who works in the off-license. He's a keen birdwatcher, he might be able to give us some advice.'

'Is he a birdwatcher?' said Florence. 'I thought he was just a pervert.'

The next morning I was up, washed and dressed at eight o'clock. I listened to the radio in the kitchen while I prepared a breakfast of porridge and coffee. One of my favourite songs came on and I sang along, quietly so as not to wake up Florence and her little friend. Socrates was asleep on the floor of her bedroom, on top of an old dressing gown. Obviously that whole cock crows at dawn thing is a load of rubbish.

When I had finished breakfast and washed up, I put my transistor radio in my rucksack, along with a flask of green tea, some chocolate and big bag of crisps. Then I was ready to go.

The supermarket was empty other than me and a couple of teenagers wandering around aimlessly, each trying to pluck up the courage to steal something, anything, simply to impress the other. Eventually one of them shoved a packet of instant mash inside his anorak and hurried towards the exit. His friend chose a tin of beans and quickly followed.

I took my groceries to the checkout, where a bored looking girl was flicking through a magazine. She gazed at me through narrowed eyes and began scanning my shopping through the till. I paid and packed everything into my rucksack, which threatened to unbalance me when I heaved it back onto my shoulders. I thanked the girl, who sneered in return, and went next door to the off-license.

A tall man with blond hair and glasses was stacking shelves with bottles of spirits. He smiled when he saw me.

'All right, Lori. Not seen you around for a while.'

'Hi Pete. How's things?'

'Not bad, you know, bit quiet what with all the snow. How are you?'

'I'm good, thanks. Listen, I was wondering if I could ask you for a bit of advice actually. You're into ornithology and all that, right?'

'That's right, Lori. You got a bird question for me?'

'Kind of. You see, we've got this rooster. It just turned up on the doorstep last night. Someone left it there, I guess. I don't know who, or why, but we can't get rid of it now. Any idea what we should do.'

'Sorry Lori,' said Pete, frowning. 'Roosters aren't really my area. I know a bloke over on the mainland though. Dave, his name is. Owns a farm. Bit mental but he's an all right fella when you get to know him. He might be able to take it off your hands. I could give him a call if you like.'

'That would be great, thanks.'

I wrote my number down on a scrap of paper. I was tempted to get a bottle of vodka but my rucksack was weighing me down enough already and I didn't want to add any more to the load. When I got home Florence was in the kitchen preparing lunch. Soup and homemade bread.

'I won't have any of that,' I said. 'Wheat intolerance.'

'But you had that cake. That must have had flour in it.'

'No, that was... special flour.'

I unpacked the shopping and we sat at the kitchen table to eat, Socrates watching us from the corner. I told Florence about Dave and his farm. She shrugged and started to hack into the bread.

'You don't seem very happy about it,' I said.

'No, it's good news. I just, you know, was becoming quite attached.'

'To a rooster?'

'I know it's stupid. But I've never had a pet before. And he follows me everywhere. It's like he's adopted me.'

'You're right. That is stupid.'

'Lori...'

'Sorry. But look, we could get a budgie or something. How about that?'

'What about a pig?'

On Monday morning we wrapped Socrates in a blanket and set off. Peter was going to travel to the mainland with us, where we would meet Dave. On the boat, Florence sat with her arms wrapped protectively around the bundle on her lap, while Pete and I threw pennies into the water.

'What happens to the chickens on Dave's farm?' I whispered.

'Oh, they're very happy,' Pete whispered back. 'Yeah, they have very happy lives.'

'And then?'

'And then...' He grinned, then drew his hand across his throat in a slicing motion. I felt slightly queasy.

'Right. Don't tell me anymore.' I turned to Florence. 'I've changed my mind.'

'What do you mean?'

'About the farm. I don't think it's the right place for Socrates. We'll find somewhere else. He can stay with us in the meantime.'

'Ok,' said Florence happily. 'Sounds good to me.'

'Sorry about this,' I told Pete. 'I really appreciate your help. I just can't do it.'

'No worries. So, do you fancy going out sometime?' He leaned in close. 'To say thank you.'

'No offence Pete, but I would rather die.'

'Fair enough.'

When we got back home there was a note taped to the front door.

Thank you for looking after my rooster. I will collect him some time in the next 24 hours. Please await further instructions.

'Well, what does *that* mean?' I said.

We waited up all night, Florence pacing up and down the hallway, trying to work out who might have left the note. As time passed we got more and more anxious. We should never have brought the damn rooster into the house.

The sun was just starting to rise when there was a knock on the door. We stood, frozen, staring at one another. Another knock. Florence took a step back.

'I just remembered,' she said. 'It's your turn to answer the door.'

126

Featherblade

STEPHEN MCQUIGGAN

THREE WEEKS LATER and the parrot still hadn't spoken. Vic regarded it as he ate and the bird returned his suspicious stare. Blushing, he turned his back on it and carried his plate over to the kitchen sink. The bird was starting to get to him. He had bought it for companionship, but now it's stubborn refusal to speak seemed to him a form of contempt. He could feel its eye upon him as he washed his hands. The thought was completely ridiculous, but still... wasn't that Heather's eye? Endowed with the very same glare of scorn that she bestowed on him every time he stuffed his face.

Heading back to the table he snatched a lamp and, flicking the switch, turned it on the parrot so that its gaudy colours shone like the war-paint of a savage.

'You're gonna talk before this is all over,' he said, 'You're gonna sing like a canary.' Smiling to himself, he turned to share the joke but the kitchen was empty. The house was empty. Heather was gone. He felt hungry again. Taunting him, the parrot grabbed a grape from the dish by its perch and flicked its delicate tongue around it. Vic shivered. It was as if the feathers were a costume draped over the monster beneath, a monster you could still glimpse in those cold, doll eyes and in those razor claws. A claw that could hold a grape so gently and so firmly could just as easily pop an eyeball. Vic wondered if he should have bought a puppy instead, but puppies didn't talk.

As he stared, the bird ducked its head to one side as if patronising him with its attention, a gesture so familiar to him that his eyes blurred over with tears.

'Heather?'

He had to get a grip on himself. Heather was gone. He went to the fridge and took out a block of cheese, chewing on it before he had even closed the door. A tiny wisp of a girl was Heather Wade, what would she think if she could see him now? Vic Harris – half man, half mattress. Once, whilst waddling down Silver Street, a couple of little brats had walked behind him mimicking his ungainly lope.

'Hey Mister!' they shouted, 'Are you the see-saw champion of the world?' He rarely went out anymore.

He knew that in her smug, silent way Heather would mock his weight gain. When they had first met he had clung to her, clutched her close to him, terrified she would fly away; and she had, with a guy called Norman from her fitness class. Now he thought of her trim body as an illness, a bony uncertainty, a symbol of the famine in her scruples. When she left he stockpiled forbidden dairy products, hoarded desserts, in a spurt of glorious rebellion. Each pound gained was a flabby victory but one that rendered him, a slave to gravity, unable to fly after her.

His gums singing from the last of the cheese he walked into the hall, pausing before the mirror. 'Who's a pretty boy then?' His smile was unnecessary as he now possessed the common or garden variety fat, happy face. He would call her, 'Heather, I need you' and she would come. He picked up the phone then set it down again, repeating the action over and over until he caught sight of his hand gripping the sweaty receiver, the knuckles white and angry, the finger with no ring, no tourniquet for loneliness. He dropped the phone.

'Please, please... someone... someone just ring!' He could hear the parrot flapping its wings in panic in the kitchen. He hated it even more when it did that, the dislodged air smelt like her perfume. He went upstairs muttering to himself, 'Greasy, camp crow.'

By the time he reached the top he was out of breath. His panting froze as he heard a muffled chatter coming from his bedroom. He relaxed when he realised he had left the television on. The musty air in his disheveled room was almost too thick to breathe, it stuck to his skin like half-sucked toffee, as he bent to switch off the portable.

He had taken to sleeping with it on a few months ago, just before he had bought the bird. At night it dowsed his sleeping face in flickering primary colours that pervaded his dreams. He slept through disasters, car chases and the crash of stock markets. He awoke to massacres and deadly new viruses. The parrot liked the news, watched it all the time. But no more. Vic was wise to its little game, he knew it only watched it because she –

The phone rang.

Vic felt a serpent writhe in his belly as something acrid surfed up his throat. *Someone ringing me? Heather?*

He grabbed the doorknob. It slid through the sweaty sausages of his fingers. He forced himself to stop and wipe his hands on his egg stained T-shirt, which was beginning to resemble the Turin shroud, and count to ten before descending the stairs. A strange fear assailed him, his eagerness to answer the persistent ring fading with every step.

What if the phone bared its teeth and tore off his hand? The wrist bone protruding from his candy coloured flesh like a message in a bottle. Help! I am shipwrecked in my own life. The phone was sleek and shiny, just like her. It was false and plastic with an irritating chirpy voice. The phone was all that kept him connected. The phone was off the hook.

It dangled from its umbilical cord where he had dropped it, a faint hum issuing from its metallic mouth. Through the kitchen door he could see the parrot staring at him. 'You?' Could parrots impersonate a ringing phone? Was it really playing with his mind the way she used to? He rubbed away the sweat that stung his eyes as he strode into the kitchen. He didn't want the bird to think he had been crying, that it had won. 'No news for you today' he said as he lurched past it on his way to the fridge to get an apple tart.

He caught sight of his neighbour, Jenny, hanging out some washing, framed in his window. Jenny was in love with him and, if he was honest, he had a bit of a crush on her too. She wasn't much to look at, single mum and all, but it was her plainness that attracted him. That type wasn't likely to stray. He watched her bend over, her mouth full of pegs, and conceded that she was a tad on the large side, her body built for comfort not for speed. Vic smiled, already wondering what his next excuse was to call. He had already exhausted the coffee route.

The dripping tap broadened that smile, water, perfect. People used a lot of water. He would have to call on her several times a day. He tittered at his cunning.

Leaving the kitchen he walked past the living room and saw the parrot perched on the edge of the settee gazing at the dormant television. 'Not a chance' he said with malicious glee, 'No news for you. Nevermore.' He was still laughing as he stepped out his front door.

Jenny's door was red and this made him hungry. As he approached it all he could think of was steak. When he got hungry he got nervous and when he got nervous he sweated profusely. By the time Jenny answered he was floundering on her doorstep like a castaway. Her face folded into a frown upon seeing him. Vic put this down to the fact that she was an unmarried mother. People like that were always frowning, perhaps that's why they weren't married.

'Yes?' Her voice was tense and her nose wrinkled up as if offended by some awful stench. The baby's just filled its nappy, reasoned Vic. He ran a hand over his head to smooth down his greasy curls.

'Hi Jenny, listen ah... I'm sorry to bother you but my water's off and I was wondering if I could borrow –'

'So's mine.' It was too quick, the look on her face showed she knew it.

'Excuse me?'

'I said so's mine. The whole street's probably off. They must have hit a pipe or something. I expect it'll be on again soon though.' She hesitated, wary to test the limits of her courage, 'Goodbye.' She closed the door firmly leaving Vic with his mouth open, trying to come to terms with what had happened.

Her water was off ? The lying bitch!

He was shocked at the level of her deceit. The ugly, fat bitch, he was only trying to do her a favour. What guy in his right mind would want her anyway, what with her being saddled with a brat and another one on the way by the look of it. No, it would never have worked anyway, on top of everything else she had a cat.

Back home he found the parrot had not moved. Might as well be stuffed he thought, as he watched it gaze at the dead screen. He trudged to the sink and poured himself a glass of water, watching as Jenny returned to her washing. Waiting until he caught her eye, he raised his glass and toasted her mockingly. She reddened and hurried back inside.

Making himself a sandwich he rejoined the parrot, feeling the bread crumble to dust in his mouth as the bird turned to face him. 'Okay, okay, I know what you want.' He turned on the television, daubing mayonnaise over the remote control as he surfed the channels until he found the rolling news one the bird was so fascinated by. 'She'll be on soon.' He said.

He leaned back, ready to take a bite out of his rejuvenated snack, when the doorbell went. *Heather?* he got up as quickly as he could, tore open the front door like a prize winning envelope. It was Jenny and she looked angry, the type of angry you rehearse.

'Listen Rick.'

'It's Vic,' he broke in, but this seemed to make her more determined.

'Vic...' I'm having trouble getting little Miles to sleep at night, what with all your singing and – '

'Excuse me?' Vic was at a loss, what the hell was she talking about? *Could it be that the parrot, I mean she's angry enough for it to be true, could it be that the parrot was*

'Singing, all bloody night and I've had enough, it has to stop. It's harassment for one thing, it's – '

'It's the parrot.' said Vic, almost to himself.

'What?'

'My parrot. He sings all night, all day too probably. But don't worry, I'm working on a plan that'll fix him good.' She stared at him, a mixture of disbelief and disgust stewing in her eyes. Vic was getting excited now, soon he would be able to slam the door on *her*. 'Anything else?' It was all he could do not to laugh in her horrible mousy face.

'Well, actually...' It was obvious she was steeling herself, she blushed as she took the plunge. 'There's been, um... well... some of my panties have been... disappearing off my line. I was wondering if perhaps you'd seen anything?' She sounded almost apologetic.

'Probably the parrot again,' offered Vic.

'The parrot?' She looked genuinely stumped, as if she might cry, 'Why would a parrot do something like that?'

'Dunno. Maybe it was abused as an egg.' He closed the door, laughing as he returned to the living room. The parrot was watching the news with the kind of concentration Vic usually reserved for seafood. He felt a sudden fondness for the bird, a wave of jovial camaraderie sweep over him. 'So you can sing then can you? You kept that quiet.' He chuckled as he finished his sandwich. 'Don't worry, she'll be on soon.' He said in lieu of a peace offering.

He watched the bird for a long time, as wars and oil strikes played themselves out over 28 inches on his wall. The smile slipped from his face like a slug from a dog bowl. 'You're not Heather, are you?' The parrot sat, and stared, and nothing more. He felt an all consuming hunger envelop him. 'I'll go and make a feed then we can watch her together.' He got up to prepare the last supper.

But he could not rustle up the energy to cook, so instead he grabbed some lollipops from the freezer. He had eaten so many lately that his tongue had taken on a chemical hue, and he sometimes imagined a bad joke to be written down his spine. He returned just as she was coming on. Her name was Heather too, Heather the weather. The parrot was obsessed with her.

It was all a form of witchcraft, he mused, as he watched her amid the little marshmallow clouds. She moved her hands constantly, in a strange flapping motion, to emphasise her words. They looked like plucked and dying birds. Her hair obliterated Scotland, her face a ghastly orange as if she had strayed too close to the sun. She'll burn her wings one day, he thought, burn her wings and fall. There was no fear in her doll-like eyes, eyes that were ignorant of her inhuman smile. Her clothes, her gaudy plumage, revealed she was hollow down to her bones.

And she was a liar.

Just like his fair-weather wife. Just like Jenny. He turned away from her breezy optimism to look outside. The day had become a monochrome soak despite her forecast. 'There'll be no more lily liars in this house.' He said, switching off the television, 'There are going to be a few changes my fine feathered friend, quite a few.' Vic was suddenly aware that he smelt bad, it accosted him as he struggled to get up. He would not have been surprised to have seen gulls circling him. There was a hair on the end of his lolly, and he felt like crying because it had been in his mouth, and if you swallowed a hair it turned into a wriggly worm.

What kind of boy went around with worms in his belly? The kind of boy who would marry that no good, hungry looking Heather Wade, that's what kind, that's exactly what kind. Mummy always told him things like that. Mummy always kept him right. If you cut yourself on barbed wire you would be poisoned and die. If you were stung by a nettle, the little white lumps would suck all the blood away from your heart. If you got bitten by a dog you would turn into one (*You're father was bitten by a dog Victor, a great big wolf of a thing*) and, if you kissed a girl, you would never be happy again. Heather had kissed him like a nettle and now his heart was dead.

The parrot was flapping wildly around the room, seen through his tears it was just a smear of colour. 'Are you going to leave me too!' he yelled as the feathers dropped like snow around him. The parrot made a final swoop then flew headlong into the window, a feathered bomb, an explosion of reds and greens, then silence. An awful silence after the dull thump of impact. There was a crack on the pane like a wishbone.

Vic felt a scream rise like bile from the depths of his gut, a scream that would shatter that silence into a million tiny pauses. Terror clutched at him as he approached the little broken body. Terror was not the blow of a sledgehammer, but rather, the deft, swift plunge of a feather blade, thin and lethal. The bird lay marooned on an island of its own blood. Its eye flicked open briefly, regarding him in the old way, before closing again.

'Heather,' it said.

Snow Baby

SUSAN EVERETT

S HE HAD THAT dream again. The one where the
sky is burning and the house is on fire. Where her
mother drags her by the hand through smoke to the outside, her own hand gripped around a doll. Outside, to
brightness, uniforms, people. And she's shouting for her
Grandmother. Babcia! Babcia! And she sees her come out
of the building, flames behind, face grey with soot, but
smiling.

'I'm alive!'

And the house topples and falls, and Babcia disappears
beneath it.

How she needed Babcia now.

She looked down at her belly, a pink layer of skin with
a secret underneath. It looked rounder than normal. She
sucked in her breath to try to reduce the size, but all it did
was make her dizzy. She wanted to hit it, bounce it out,
like she'd tried months before, when she thudded down
the stairs on her rump, carpet burns biting her legs. It
wouldn't go. Nor would it go when she drank half a bottle of gin and sank into a boiling bath. When she fainted
and cracked the bathroom tiles with her forehead.

The scar would never go.

She sank back onto the narrow bed in the small room that wasn't hers. Downstairs the English family that wasn't hers would soon be having breakfast, and she would go down and try to swallow a teaspoon of boiled egg or a spoon of stodgy porridge. Then she would offer to wash up, be declined, and would come upstairs again. Mrs Trask would smile at her, a sad smile, apologetic, with that look across her face, the one that said *I'm glad you're not my daughter*.

* * *

1944: Twenty years before, and the whole of Warsaw was burning. Babcia never made it outside the house, she was still inside while the flames took hold.

'Babcia!'

And she herself, a small child, struggling for release from her mother's hand, spinning underneath her arm. Slipping free and running home to help.

'Babcia!'

Stopped by the barrel of a gun pointed at her, with the disinterested face of an SS officer standing behind. She only came up to his knees.

Walking, walking, as they were herded up the burning streets, her mother's hand so tight on hers it made her numb inside. Hundreds walking. Human cattle guided along by men and tanks under a sky that snowed black ash. Past a hospital, ablaze, its patients locked inside on burning mattresses. Past a woman walking on all fours like a dog, her clothes smoking, her red hair still on fire.

Walking, walking, as she did right now, counting footsteps in her head to match her heartbeat. Walking through Arnos Park, cold biting at her cheeks while the baby kicked inside her.

Kick.

And her thoughts still back in Poland. Walking towards the station, where they were herded onto trains. Packed so tight she found it hard to breathe. Her mother rubbed the top of her head to keep her calm. They stopped at a field hospital, and felt fresh air again.

She knew now, as a young adult of twenty five, that this was where it could have ended. That if her mother hadn't recently had her appendix out, if she didn't still have the dressing on, if the Polish doctor hadn't seen, they would have stayed on the train to Auschwitz. Instead they were pulled off into the makeshift hospital, where the wound was to be re-dressed before they were put on the next morning's transport. Her mother slept on a camp-bed, while she lay on the floor beneath. The doctor came over in the dark and nudged them, told them to be quiet. To follow him, out, out of the camp towards the trees. He pointed into the blackness and told them they should run.

Into the woods she ran. She ran. Holding her mother's hand. Bumping into branches and thick roots until daylight took hold. Every day became the same: walking, hiding, eating berries, stealing from fields. Washing hands in muddy puddles, drying them with crispy leaves. Listening for distant gunfire and other human sounds. Sleeping underneath the trees while her mother read the stars and told her stories from before the world went bad. And she walked, walked, her mother leading, heading south for Krakow, the place where hope still lived. As the snow began to fall, she caught white flakes on her tongue and smiled as they fizzed into cold water.

And all the time she walked.

She walked.

* * *

She had her baby on a Monday, after the nuns went off to mass as her waters broke. The tea lady heard her screaming and stayed to hold her hand. The other girls hid in their rooms, with their fake names and big bellies filled with babies ready to burst. Babies that would be laid out in a row of cots, for inspection by prospective parents. Married couples, Catholics, who would save them from their sin.

Her baby was going to a couple in Hertfordshire. Next week.

She walked across the grounds, with her tiny daughter wrapped up warmly, clutched against her breast. Mumbling, with bubbles popping from her mouth. They weren't meant to go outside, especially now, in the cold, the snow. She hadn't meant to. She only meant to look. But as her shadow fell across the cot her baby twitched her nose and seemed to smile. So she picked her up and before she knew it, was down the corridor and outside.

Fresh air against her face felt like a shock, like she was waking up. She'd not stopped to get a coat, but the shivering made her stronger. She looked down at her daughter, with eyes matching her own. She held her tight, like that doll she'd never lost. Her mother had held her hand, now she was holding hers.

She trudged across the white expanse of lawn towards the woods on the horizon.

And she walked.

She walked.

The Day They Took My Dad Away

DAVID T HAY

IT WASN'T TOO hard to call the ambulance this time but it was a real shock that they turned up with a camera crew. At first I thought that they were making a training video but in the end it turned out that they were making a TV show about the ambulance people.

Dad had only consumed vodka and cigarette smoke for over a week now. Worse than that, he hadn't moved from his mattress in front of the TV and I knew that the house smelled bad but I'd gotten used to it. Of course, I didn't really like the camera crew being there. People who see my dad usually behave in a similar way. First they are shocked, like they've walked into a glass door, and then they look at me with pity. Then they're shocked again and it's like they blame me for the state that my old man's in. Then it switches back to pity again.

The fella with the camera was straight in there. He was funny to watch. He would film for a little while, all still and crouched and careful. Then he would spring into life and march to the other side of the room and crouch again, just like a cat stalking a bird. The ambulance man kept talking to the camera but he didn't really say anything. But they didn't really do anything either.

The pretty girl that was with the cameraman didn't come inside. She stood in the doorway and called me over. She talked to me about what they were doing and asked me to sign a form. She asked me if it was my house and I said it was. She asked me how long I had let my father stay for and she seemed really surprised when I said that it was his house too and that we had always lived together. Then she asked me to sign another form then she told me not to worry and that they probably wouldn't use what they filmed anyway.

They took his pulse and then his blood pressure and then they picked him up and put him on their little chair with wheels that can fold out into a stretcher. I don't know why they make such a fuss. Dad is so skinny I could just about carry him with one hand. It was when they picked him up that the cameraman ran out of the house and wretched in the driveway. Then he apologised to me and went back inside. He filmed them taking dad out and asked the ambulance men to explain what they were doing and why. They put him in the ambulance and the cameraman went back inside and started filming the living room. He filmed the sheets, the mattress, dad's mess on the carpet, the pile of cigarette stubs, the empty vodka bottles. As I watched him filming the vodka bottles they suddenly struck me as quite beautiful. They were so clean amongst all that filth and they were glinting in the sunlight. Then he filmed the TV, the stereo, the ornaments, the pictures on the wall – all sorts of stuff, from all sorts of angles. The girl called him over and they stepped outside and talked for a moment. The cameraman came over to me and introduced himself with a smile and asked how I was feeling. Just as I started to answer he raised the camera up and started filming me. He asked me about my dad and how long he had been an alcoholic for. He asked me if it had been hard to call the ambulance and have him taken away and then he poked his head out from behind the camera and looked at me and nodded with a sympathetic frown on his face. He asked if this had happened before and if this was the worst he had been, then he stopped and thought for a minute. He smiled and said that I seemed like a really normal young guy and that when he looked around the house he was struck by how clean it was apart from the spot where my dad was but he trailed off and I didn't answer because it wasn't really a question.

The House Next Door

JOHN TODD

A T LAST, THINGS were beginning to quieten down again. There had been a period of renewed interest in the house, when the trial had begun. The jury had been brought to see it, though Clare could not understand why, since there could be little doubt about what had happened, and surely there was nothing these people could be shown that could make any difference to their verdict.

She had watched them emerge from the house. They had stood around outside, before getting back into the bus that had brought them. One man was trying to make light of things, but no one was listening. A woman was in tears. An older woman had an arm around her, trying to comfort her. A third woman was being sick. Clare's heart went out to these people. She remembered her own feelings of horror and disgust when she first heard what had happened (and she had not had to go down into the cellar, as these people had).

Later, the press had been back, and the television people. And, in the evening, there was the house on the box again, with the same reporter standing in front of it, talking into his mike, and their own house just visible to one side.

The sightseers had also reappeared. Cars had stopped, and their occupants had sat for long periods, staring idiotically at the house. Sometimes they had got out and taken photographs.

At least, this time, she and Simon had not been troubled directly. There had been no more interviews with the police, and no reporters ringing their doorbell, wanting to know what they could tell them about the Murgesses. (She had said, truthfully, that they had had little to do with their neighbours. The Murgesses had been people who 'kept themselves to themselves'. Widowed Mrs Johnson, on the other side, enjoying the attention, had been more forthcoming.)

Now all was quiet again. The trial went on, but it was no longer in the news, some other sensational event having taken its place. There were fewer sightseers, some days none at all. Things were almost back to normal. But Clare felt things could not be normal again.

'I want to move,' she said to Simon. 'I don't want to live in this house any more. I don't want Ellie and Sam to grow up here.'

'We can't move,' he said. 'Not at the moment. Who would buy this place right now?'

'Someone might,' she said. 'Someone who didn't know.'

'They'd find out soon enough. It would come out long before they signed the contract.'

'We could drop the price,' she said. 'Someone might be glad to get a house like this cheap.'

'We can't afford to drop the price, love. When we move, we'll want something bigger, for when the kids grow up. We'll need to get as much for this place as we can. Sorry, we're going to have to stay here another year at least.'

Clare said, 'I don't want Ellie to know what happened.'

'She might never find out.'

'She will, if we're here another year. At present, she thinks the Murgesses have gone to live somewhere else. That's what I told her. But she'll be four next year, she'll be starting school. The other kids'll say something to her, then she'll find out the whole thing.'

'Would it matter so much?'

'Of course it would matter! Can't you imagine the effect on her, when she hears the horrible details? And realises she was just a few yards away when it happened? She could have nightmares for years. It could affect her whole life.'

'Well, at least it shouldn't trouble Sam,' said Simon. 'We should be long gone by the time he's old enough to understand.'

Clare said, 'If we could move somewhere in the next few months, Ellie need never find out what happened. She'd only have a vague memory of this house, and probably wouldn't remember the Murgesses at all.'

'That would be a good thing, obviously.'

'So let's put the house on the market, and see what happens. You never know, we might get a buyer.'

'Okay, we'll give it a try.'

So, the next day, they called at an estate agents, and their house was put up for sale. A sign was erected in their front garden, and an advertisement appeared in a local paper, with a photograph. Clearly visible in the photograph was the house next door.

Meanwhile, that house stood empty. One night, someone broke all its windows, either as a random act of vandalism or an expression of outrage at what had happened. Next day, workmen came and boarded up the openings. Clare wondered how long the building would remain unoccupied. She could see it slowly deteriorating, the paint peeling, the woodwork eventually rotting. The garden was already overgrown, the paths disappearing under weeds.

For a long time, no one came to look at their own house. It seemed that Simon might be right, that no one wanted to live next door to the place where that awful thing had happened. Then, one day, the agent brought a young couple round. They seemed pleased with the house, the wife especially. She enthused about the kitchen, the bathroom, the garden. Shortly afterwards, another couple came. They too appeared to like the house. There seemed every chance that at least one of these couples would make an offer. But weeks passed, and nothing more was heard from either of them.

'They found out about next door,' Clare said.

The garden of the empty house became more overgrown. Brambles arched across flower beds, ivy began to envelop Harold Murgess's greenhouse. The garden became a hunting-ground for the neighbourhood cats. Once Clare heard the squealing of a caught and tormented mouse.

One morning, she noticed that a door of the empty house was wide open. Someone, a thief or souvenir-hunter, had broken in. She rang the police. Next day, a workman nailed heavy planks across all the doorways. The house was now more of an eyesore than ever. Clare longed for it to be pulled down.

Ellie had her fourth birthday. Clare arranged a small party, to which half-a-dozen children were invited. Only three came, the mothers of the others finding unconvincing excuses for keeping their offspring away. Clare wondered what these women were afraid of. Did they think their little ones might come to some harm, because of something that had happened in an adjoining house, more than a year before?

Ellie was troubled. She could not understand why her friend Amanda had not come to the party. She seemed unconvinced that Amanda had a cold.

Next day, she announced, 'Mummy, something bad happened next door.'

Clare thought, she's found out. Trying to appear unconcerned, she said, 'Oh, yes, dear? What happened? Tell me about it.'

Ellie frowned, and did not reply. Evidently, she had heard something she had not understood.

The year came to an end. No one else had been to look at their house. The agent said not many people were house hunting at that time of year. But he was confident that he would find a buyer for them in the spring.

One afternoon, a young man appeared at the door. Clare's heart sank when she saw him. She thought he was another reporter, come to trouble them with more questions about the Murgesses. But the young man nodded towards the FOR SALE sign, and asked if he might look round the house. Clare, holding the baby in her arms, said she was sorry, all inspections had to be done through the agent. The young man said, yes, he understood that, and he would of course get in touch with the agent later, but would she mind if he had a quick look first – just to get some idea what the place was like? Clare was not keen to let in a stranger when Simon was not there, but the young man seemed harmless, and she felt she could not let the chance of a possible sale slip through her fingers. She invited him in.

She deposited Sam in his playpen, then took the young man round and showed him each of the rooms. It soon became clear that he was not greatly interested in what he saw. He appeared to have something else on his mind. Clare began to worry. She wished now that she had not asked him in.

Unexpectedly, the young man asked to see the garden. Clare thought, he's a keen gardener. It's the garden he's really interested in.

Relieved, she opened the French doors, and led him outside. She showed him round, pointing out the garden's best features. 'It looks a picture in the spring,' she told him. The young man made a show of being impressed, but was plainly not interested. His attention kept straying to the house next door.

'It's been empty a long time,' Clare said. 'We're hoping someone will buy it and do it up.'

The young man gazed at the ugly, empty house.

'I expect you knew the people who lived there quite well,' he said.

'Not really. They were the sort who kept themselves to themselves. Look, you're not really interested in buying our house, are you?'

The young man laughed.

'All right, I admit it.' He took a notebook from his pocket. 'I'm writing a book about the Murgesses. I expect you could tell me a few things about them.' He grinned at her. 'I wasn't sure you'd let me in, if I said that was what I wanted. I gather you weren't too keen to talk to the press boys.'

'That's because I had nothing to tell them!' she said, angrily. 'And that goes for you, too. Now will you leave, please.'

150

'Just a few details,' he said. 'I won't take up much of your time.'

'I repeat – I've got nothing to tell you!' she said. 'If you want to know more about the Murgesses, go and speak to Mrs Johnson on the other side.'

'I already have...'

'Can't you understand?' she said. 'We're trying to forget we ever knew the Murgesses. We want to be normal people living normal lives. We don't want people like you pestering us. Now will you please go away.' She indicated a narrow path that ran down the side of their house. 'You can get out that way,' she said.

She went back into the house, closing the French doors behind her.

She was confronted by Ellie.

'Mummy, what does the man want?'

'Nothing, dear. He was just asking a lot of silly questions.'

'Why are you cross with him?'

'Because he told a lie. We shouldn't tell lies, should we?'

'Why did he tell a lie?'

'Never mind, dear. Now, you were going to help me with my ironing, weren't you? Which pile needs ironing? Is it this one?'

Ellie said, 'The man's in the garden, Mummy.'

'What?'

Clare spun round. The young man was standing by the fence, peering into the Murgesses' garden. He was making notes in his notebook.

She flung open the French doors.

'I thought I told you to go away!' she shouted.

The young man hesitated, then, with a resigned grin, pocketed his notebook and headed for the side of the house. Clare did not trust him. She made her way to a front window, to make sure he was leaving. She watched him get into his car and drive away.

Ellie had followed her to the window.

'The man came about that bad thing,' she said.

'What bad thing?'

Again, Ellie frowned and said nothing. Clare was deeply worried. How much did the child know?

She began the ironing. Following their usual practice, Ellie handed her items to be ironed, then took them from her when she had finished. The little girl was very quiet. Clare wondered what was going on in her daughter's mind.

Eventually, Ellie said, 'Mummy.'

'Yes, dear?'

'Where are Mr and Mrs Murgess?'

'I told you, dear. They've gone to live somewhere else.'

'Where?'

'I don't know.'

'Why did they go? Was it because of that bad thing?'

'What bad thing? You keep talking about a bad thing.'

She waited for a reply, but none came. Exasperated, she resumed her ironing.

Ellie said, 'The man was asking about Mr and Mrs Murgess.'

Clare said, sharply, 'How do you know that?'

Ellie began to cry. Clare put an arm round her.

'I'm sorry, love,' she said. 'I didn't mean to shout. Let's forget about Mr and Mrs Murgess, shall we? They've gone and they won't be coming back. Maybe some new people will come and live in their house. They might have a little girl like you. That would be nice, wouldn't it?'

Ellie stopped crying, and thought about this. The idea must have appealed to her. She seemed to forget about the 'bad thing', her mind now being full of the little girl she believed was coming to live next door. Later, she asked Clare, 'When will these people come, Mummy? The people with the little girl?'

The trial came to an end at last. The jury reached the expected verdict (what other verdict could there be?), and sentence was passed, the heaviest sentence possible. The newspapers again had a field day, as did the broadcasting companies, but this time there were no television cameras outside the house, and no sightseers came to stare.

But the house still stood, amid its wilderness of weeds and scattered rubbish. In March, a fierce wind blew some slates off the roof, and a tree came down in the back garden. Nobody did anything about it. Clare thought, the house will become derelict, and the garden a jungle. And, even if someone bought the place and restored it, it would still have its horrid associations. More than ever, she longed to get away.

No one came to look at their own house. It seemed they would have to remain there forever. And, all the time, Ellie was becoming brighter, more observant. Clare thought, I shan't be able to keep the truth from her much longer. Sooner or later, she's going to find out what happened next door.

The young man's book came out. With the trial and the verdict fresh in people's minds, it was an instant bestseller. Extracts appeared in a popular daily newspaper. There was talk of it being made into a film.

Everyone was talking about the case. Time and again, Clare heard the name 'Murgess' – in the shops, on the bus, in the street. She thought, Ellie is sure to hear. Any time now, she will start asking questions again. What shall I tell her?

No questions came, but Ellie was silent for long periods, as if turning something over in her mind. She no longer asked about the little girl who was coming to live next door.

If only, Clare thought, someone would come along and buy our house now. We might just be able to get away before Ellie finds out the truth.

One afternoon, returning from a visit to the shops, she saw three people, two men and a young woman, emerge from the garden of the house next door. Her first thought was that they were up to no good. Then she noticed that they were respectably, even smartly, dressed. They were carrying equipment of some sort. They bundled it into the boot of a car, and drove off.

She wondered what was going on. She remembered the talk of a film being made about the Murgesses. Surely they didn't intend to shoot it here? Dismayed, she saw the house becoming a centre of attention again, with sightseers gaping from their cars, and people ringing their doorbell, wanting to ask them questions. Why, she thought, can't people forget about this dreadful business? Surely, everything that could be said about the Murgesses has been said by now?

A few weeks later, an official-looking envelope arrived in the post. Simon opened it, and said, 'Hey, look at this!'

'What is it?' said Clare.

'It's from the Council,' he said. 'Someone's made an application to knock down the Murgesses' house and build two new houses in its place.'

'What!'

She hurried to his side, and they studied the documents together. Drawings showed two neat little houses standing between their own house and Mrs Johnson's. Nothing could have looked less like the ugly building that occupied the site at present.

'These will look great,' said Simon. 'And look, there's landscaping! See those shrubs? When all this has been done, there'll be nothing left of what was there before. People will forget this is where it happened. They'll remember the event, but they won't connect it with this place.'

And so it turned out, almost. It took a long time for the planning application to go through, then for the site to be cleared, and for the new houses to be built. But, when they were up, it was as Simon had predicted. They looked good, fitted snugly in the site, and harmonised well with the houses on either side. It was as if nothing else had ever stood on the site.

Clare and Simon now began to get offers for their own house, but, strangely, found themselves reluctant to sell. There seemed no strong reason for moving, now that the Murgesses' house no longer stood next door. Also, their new neighbours were friendly, and, as it turned out, had a little girl about Ellie's age, unexpectedly fulfilling Clare's prophecy. They felt as if they had already moved – no further move seemed necessary. Simon rang the estate agent, and told him they had decided to stay after all. The next day, the FOR SALE sign was removed from their front garden.

* * *

Ellie had started school while the new houses were being built. On her first day, Clare walked with her to the school. They set off together, Ellie helping push Sam in the buggy. Clare was full of apprehension about what her daughter might learn at the school. How much would the other children know? She tried telling herself that this was only an infants' school, and that surely the parents of four and five year olds would, like herself, have prevented their little ones from finding out about the horrific thing that had happened so close to their homes. With luck, she thought, Ellie will remain in ignorance for another year at least.

It was a vain hope. Some of the children starting school that year already knew what had happened, and, within a few days, so did all the others. Ellie had long known that something very bad had happened in the house next door. Now she learned the full, gruesome details. She sobbed, in misery and terror.

But her distress soon gave way to feelings of a different kind. She was rapidly identified as 'the girl who lived next door', and found herself regarded with respect, even awe, by the other children. She was quick to take advantage of this. She pretended she had known all along what had happened. She was pleased when other children came and asked her about it. She told them everything she knew, adding a few details which she had made up. Soon her story bore little resemblance to the truth, but it was believed.

She went on telling it when she moved to her next school. She was an awkward, unattractive little girl, not good at joining in games, and, in the normal way of things, she would not have been popular with the other children. But she had her story, and, whenever she wanted attention, she could tell it. Everyone listened, agog, as she told them what had happened in the house next door.

The Archaeologist's Wife

DAVID PESCOD

B ILL MARKS OUT a space in the garden as I watch through the misty kitchen window. I hold my mug, clenching the last warmth, and top it up when he comes in for breakfast.

'Aren't you dressed yet?' He asks.

No good morning, no peck on the cheek, no cuddle. He rushes his breakfast, breaking the shell as he scrapes out the last of the boiled egg, and dashes upstairs with a yoke stained chin, shouting as he goes. 'I suppose you don't have to get dressed, now you've slung in the library job. You'll miss the routine. Still, you know best.' He descends with his new gardening gloves.

'Any chance of more tea?' He asks on his way out.

It must be serious, if he's using the Alan Titchmarsh gloves, advertised in the Radio Times.

We took the Eurostar through the tunnel for a long weekend last year. It was the counsellor's idea, a final resort. We did the usual things, but he insisted we saw the Catacombs, miles of tunnels with skulls and bones. Six million Parisians, stacked in an orderly fashion, like a death supermarket. That's where Bill's mug came from.

New projects start every day, and he's lost interest in the vegetable patch. But he still puts some produce by the road on the little table, for beer money. He wraps them up so carefully in clear plastic bags, all priced, by the terracotta jug for the money. It upset him last week. Someone nicked the small change and urinated in the jug, but left the vegetables.

I put the kettle on again, a peppermint tea bag in his mug, and another red label one in the pot for me. I've tried to reach out for him in the night but he turns away, rolling into a ball. It's years now that we've slept in the same bed but dreamt of other people and other places. Our house has become a museum, where exhibits can't be touched and I am on display as a human, next to the carp Bill caught and stuffed when he had his taxidermy phase.

I tap on the window, and put his mug outside on the sill. He waves as if he is a tourist in another country. I close the window to stop the draught, and the sound of his whistling.

My mug begins to warm, and I think of Alan at the library, when he ran his hand up my skirt. We were tidying the storeroom together. The tingle lasted all day. I knew he fancied me, the girls had teased me for months, but I never thought a pass would come, and what followed.

'Fiction is all very well,' he said, pushing me back across the inter-library loans, 'but I'm a non-fiction man, myself.'

I go back upstairs to dress and open my wardrobe. It still looks like my mother has left her clothes in there, everything old and musty. Even though I went on that shopping spree, choosing colours that I've never worn before, gaping at the new woman in the changing room mirrors. The woman who had sex in the library store-room, interrupted by Madge looking for the kettle.

I remember her trying to smooth things over, with trifle smeared on her fat face, cheeks reddened by bad blood pressure and too much sun. Custard slid down her chin on to her summer dress.

'I didn't say anything to Mrs Pilfrey, honestly Betty.' Her podgy arms lifted some overdue books on to the trolley making more room on the desk for the trifle. She pushed it away, and began to scrape her skirt with an old library card. 'I'm a bit off my food today,' she announced.

'We're still friends, aren't we?'

I nodded, and looked away as she licked the card.

'There's a nice film on at the village hut this Friday, if you fancy it. It's that love story everyone's talking about.'

I wondered if Madge would follow me to the grave, jabbering and grazing. She lost her Ron two years ago, but she still cooks for him in her five-bedroom vicarage, laying the table for two every night and eating his portion. At least she'd still have her job at the library, something to get up for. Everybody needs to fill a hole.

That Friday, we had tea in her summerhouse with its sofa bed and rattan chairs, hidden by trees at the end of her huge garden. She let me sleep there one night, when I was thinking of leaving Bill, but I didn't tell her that. It was like a treehouse, just me with the owls at night and the flicker of flames from the woodburner throwing yellow across the pine walls. I pulled the quilt around me tight and wished I could have stayed there forever.

We set off for the film early and Madge was excited, handing out large bags of home made popcorn, and telling me all about the film.

'There are two Americans. One's loaded and the other's quite poor. They meet in a hospital tending their sick

159

partners who are dying from cancer. Well, they grieve together and then they re-appraise their lives, and guess what?'

'They have rampant sex in the Mall?'

'Not quite. But they do get it together. Touching, isn't it?' Madge put in another load of popcorn, and her eyes dwelt on this story of hope, but only for a moment before the sugar hit.

She grabbed me. 'Come on, I don't want to end up in one of those plastic bucket seats again.'

Leaning across her broken armrest, she whispered, 'I've seen him before, playing a General in Vietnam and she was in ER and that sit-com thingy. Are you sure you don't want any popcorn?'

I shook my head. Madge crunched her way through the film, but I couldn't be bothered to follow it. I woke up when the leading lady had to bare all, an advertisement for nip and tuck, and I began to wonder if a bit of Botox might bring Alan back.

Madge suddenly shrieked and the crowd shushed her. She whispered that the man next to her had tried it on, put his hand on her leg. I looked across to see a 70 year old man, struggling to blow his nose. She dragged her chair closer to me. Honey, popcorn and Madge's moisturizer filled the air.

'I wouldn't kick him out of bed,' she nodded at the screen as she regained her confidence. I watched the film star shower and recalled Alan's arse, fine and pert. But I wasn't going to share that with Madge.

That night I lay in bed, in the coffin position. I don't know if Madge did tell the head librarian, but I had been called into the main office and Mrs Pilfrey closed the door behind me, and proceeded to enforce her power. She made it pretty plain as she peered over her bifocals.

'I think it would be best if you left and used another branch of the library in future, don't you? At least till this blows over.'

Alan said his wife wasn't very well and made apologies. He was transferred to the mobile library, hard labour in Siberia. Alan has had me in many places, his car, my car, the library and in a friend's caravan. I wanted to have him here in my own home, in my own bed, or Madge's summerhouse but it won't happen now.

Bill pumps his shovel into the ground. He's been digging for days. The county archaeologists have been excavating just half a mile away.

'Roman ruins or something.' Bill says, 'there could easily be something in our garden.' I can only think of Alan's body moving back and forth, his coarse stubble against my cheek. I've taken a drug and I want more. I have many years to make up for, and I'm not interested in history.

I notice earth flying up from the hole. I can just see Bill's head rise then fall, like a piston in a steam engine, as clouds of earth puff from its funnel. I put the kettle on, and sense a chill might be coming.

The carriage clock chimes in the front room. A cruel gift to Bill, to help him watch his retirement pass. It'll go the way of most things, lining the shelves in a bric-a-brac shop, next to the old records, love songs that no one has the means to play anymore. I start humming one of those songs, drumming lightly on my mug. But, I can't quite remember the tune, and I'm left anxiously tapping.

Through the window, I see more clouds of earth rising intermittently, forming neat mounds around the hole. I don't know what Bill is looking for. Maybe he's tunnelling his way out.

Alan said we could sneak off, have a weekend away. I told him I'm an all or nothing person. He's not happy in his marriage, and his wife has affairs. He said I should be grateful that Bill isn't like that. But, I don't think he loves anybody, not anymore, not even himself. I hold my mug waiting for the warmth. The puffs of earth stop.

The hole is an almost perfect circle with small heaps of earth surrounding it, hour marks on a timepiece. I stare at Bill spread out at the bottom, face down. He is looking away from me into the ground, one arm raised, waving good-bye. His heart must have given out, it's been running on empty for too long. I pause, and slowly with my feet push the earth back into its hole, then with my hands. It seems the natural thing to do. The hole is filling, and Bill is almost covered. I push the Catacombs mug into the soft soil and start to feel warm again, sweat running down my back and hair sticking to my brow. I look up out of the hole and take a deep breath of new air. Then, my face hits the ground, as my ankle is caught by something, clasped in a grip. The earth moves, and Bill's brown face spits out wet soil. He is cursing, and pushes me down into the hole, where I struggle to get up again. A shovel hits the side of my face, and a bell rings deeper than Big Ben. I throw myself at him, full length. The gloves are off at last. We roll in the earth, more physical contact in that moment than in the last five years.

A voice calls from the house. 'Betty, are you there dear?'

We freeze and look out of our hole, as Madge's face peers over the edge. There is a long silence, and finally she coughs and makes her speech into the air.

'I came to say sorry, Betty. I feel awful about what happened. But, it's no good burying these things is it?' She throws something into the hole. I wipe my eyes to see the large brass summerhouse key lying in the fresh earth.

The Tops of
The Cupboards

GLENIS BURGESS

H E DID WHAT he did every morning. He got up and
put on his slippers and he looked out of the window. He was pleased when he saw it was a sunny day.
The clothes he would wear today – his Thursday clothes
– would keep him nice and cool. He went to the bathroom and brushed his teeth, and then washed his face
and brushed his hair. He went back to his bedroom and
put on his clothes and went downstairs.

As he walked down the stairs he could smell his cooked
breakfast in the kitchen. His wife was downstairs in the
kitchen, like she always was. He knew what his breakfast
would be as it was Thursday and all his breakfasts were
on his list. His wife needed help to get his breakfast now
and he was happy to help her. After all, she was his wife.

Because it was Thursday, his wife was wearing her
Thursday clothes, which pleased him because this was on
his list and he had helped her with them as he always did
now.

He ate his breakfast. His wife would eat later. He had
made it clear that he did not like her to eat with him. He
had made it very clear, early on, what would happen if

she ate with him again. She did not eat with him now and this pleased him and he knew that it was how she preferred it as well.

He knew how his wife would spend her day. He had written that down carefully on his list, so she could not make a mistake. She had made a mistake once, but not now, because now he wrote it all down for her. These days he always knew what his wife was doing.

Today, his wife would wash his breakfast pots and put them away in the cupboards, the right cupboards, as she did every day. Then she would clean the kitchen and, because it was Thursday, she would clean the tops of the cupboards. Once, on a Thursday, she had not cleaned the tops of the cupboards, and when he had got home that evening, he had looked at the tops of his cupboards. He had not liked what he had found and he had been displeased with his wife. But now they were always clean. He liked to know the tops of his cupboards were clean.

When she had cleaned the tops of his cupboards she would have a cup of coffee. He would make the coffee before he left. He would make it exactly as he liked it.

Then she would read a magazine until it was time for her to have lunch. Today she would have an apple and a glass of milk. He would leave the magazine and the apple and the glass of milk ready for her. He liked to know that his wife had a balanced diet in front of her.

When he came back to his house after his work, he would check the kitchen and the tops of his cupboards to see if they were clean. His wife knew he would do this. She didn't watch him do it any longer. He had shown her that he did not like her to watch him checking the tops of his cupboards, and she had not watched him since. When he had checked the tops of his cupboards he would sit down and have his dinner.

After dinner, he would read his books and then he would go to bed. His wife did not come to bed any longer. He knew she preferred to stay in the kitchen. These days he knew everything his wife thought and felt. Before he went to bed he would get her Friday clothes ready for the morning.

When he had finished his breakfast, he put his breakfast pots in his sink and washed them and put them away in his cupboards, the right cupboards, ready for Friday, and then he cleaned his kitchen and the tops of his cupboards.

He turned to his wife. As he looked at her, her head rolled backwards and her eye stared at his ceiling. He did not like it when her head rolled backwards. He would have to prop up her head. He had had to prop up her head once before and now would have to do it again. He did not think his wife had rolled her head backwards deliberately. He did not believe any longer that she deliberately did anything he did not like.

He put on his hat and went to his back door. Before he left he picked up his can of air freshener and sprayed some over his wife. He liked it when she smelt nice. He left his house and closed his door.

As he walked down his path towards his gate he thought about how he would prop up her head when he got home.

Leaving Home,
Bye-Bye

TOBY LITT

THE BEATLES SIT, left to right, George-Ringo-John-Paul, on a long pink cabriole leg sofa in Brian Epstein's house, Belgravia, answering questions after a dinner party to celebrate the release of their new album, Sgt. Pepper's Lonely Hearts Club Band. It is the 19th of May 1967. George is wearing a burgundy velvet jacket with thick stripes. Ringo is looking hip in white shirt, psychedelic tie and bespoke Edwardian-style suit with velvet trim. John is sporting a green frilly shirt, maroon trousers and a sporran. Paul has thrown on a grey pinstripe jacket, mismatched trousers and a thin silk scarf in pink and red. All The Beatles apart from Paul have moustaches. A single reporter, in grey suit, white shirt, blue tie, kneels in front of them, clutching his heavy microphone, trembling.

Paul (to reporter): The first thing I saw – in my head – were these curtains, like, with the light behind them. You know those sort of curtains. Not net curtains but not solid, either.

John: The word you're fumbling for, old chap, is cheap.

Paul: Yeah, but curtains so you can, like, see through them when there's a streetlight behind them or the sun's coming up, which is what's happening when –

George: It's five o'clock.

John: It's fab o'clonk, pomp fangs.

Paul: – when we meet the girl. It's a small house on a long terraced street, you know. Two up, two down.

John: That's a very easy crossword!

Paul: Nothing special, the house or the street. And I suppose that I was thinking, like, that she was nothing particularly special, either. The girl. I could see her, too.

John: Oh, we all saw her.

Ringo: Which girl?

George: None of us have girlfriends, apart from those of us who have wives.

Paul: I don't know where these things come from, but like they just come to me. And her I saw as, you know, a bit of a Rita Tushingham type.

John (into microphone): Hello, Rita, love. How ya doing?

Ringo: Lovely, Rita.

John: Bhagvad-rita – eh, George?

Paul: Just an ordinary girl in an ordinary house. But when I saw the morning sun coming up behind those curtains, it had a kind of sad melancholy to it.

Ringo: This is in Rita Tushingham's house? Have you been to Rita Tushingham's house?

Paul: You know, when the day hasn't quite begun but there are people up and quietly doing stuff that they don't usually do. Because she's leaving –

John: Home. Yes. And she's never going back, is she? Not to that dump.

Paul: Well...

John: Not in a million bloody years.

Ringo: What kind of curtains does Rita Tushingham have? They're not cheap, are they? She's done alright for herself, our Rita.

George: There are different kinds of light.

Paul: Yeah, George is right. They're different, even in the same house at the same time of day. Or at least, you notice them as different when you're doing something different that day.

John: Like leaving home. For ever.

Paul: And sometimes when I see pictures like that, in me head, I get the music starting up, too.

George: Funny that. Tell us more, Mr Lennon-McCartney...

Paul: I could hear it, you know, all with a slow kind of flowing, and moving from one chord to the other without you really noticing when –

John: Go on, Mendelssohn! Get in there, son!

Paul: – chord changed into the next. I like classical music.

Ringo: Is he still talking about curtains?

Paul: I've been digging a lot of, like, the classics recently. They're really cool.

John: Beethoven is a great fan of Paul's.

Paul: And I wanted some sort of grandeur to go along with this girl, as she left her girlhood behind.

John (in horror movie persona): Forever, ha ha ha!

Paul: Well, not necessarily...

George: Paul has been educating us about classical music, recently.

Ringo: Oh, aye.

Paul: I wanted the music to follow her downstairs – to sort of tiptoe out of the house with her.

John: Bye, bye, curtains.

Ringo: I like Rita Tushingham.

George: It's very sad, that bit. I think it's important that people feel these emotions, and that our music is able to make people feel them. It helps them progress.

John: And then she dances off down the road, doing a jig, because she's finally escaped –

Paul: But the song has some sympathy for –

John: Yeah, but the girl is like out of the rotten cage, isn't she? It's been all her life that she's been stuck with those twisted old people, and now she's finally free.

Ringo: I like Rita Tushingham but I like Julie Christie, too.

George: It is a kind of escape, some kind of rebirth.

Paul: Her parents aren't really equipped to understand the new world that they're living in – or, rather, you see, that their daughter wants to live in.

John: Yeah, it's hard to understand Shepherd's Bush.

George: Even shepherds don't.

John (to George): Oh, you are still there, are you? Wakely-wakely!

Paul: It hasn't been easy for their sort, going through the war and then all the gloomy stuff that came after.

John: Choosing curtains.

Paul (to John): Look, I'm trying to be serious here, alright? The man's asking me a serious question.

George: The serious man with the serious eyebrows.

Ringo: Julie Christie has a smaller nose than Rita Tushingham.

John: *You've* got a smaller nose than Rita.

Paul: Anyway, –

George (to reporter): He's not like this normally.

Ringo: I am!

George (pointing at Paul): I meant him.

Paul: When she –

John: He's *worse* than this normally.

170

Paul: – leaves the house, out the back door, goes off down the alley – when she's out, we only follow her for a while. Most of the time is spent with her mother and father. They're really making an effort to understand. I think lots of people are like that.

John: Well-meaning murderers.

Paul (to John): Look, it was me wrote the song. They're not murderers.

John (to Paul): They haven't been successful, no. But they've been trying to kill that girl since the moment she was born. There she is, alone with them in that house, and everything she does they criticize. Every boy she wants to go out with, every thought she might express, they just rip it apart, until there's almost nothing left.

Ringo: Are they at it again?

George: Another cup of tea?

Ringo: Don't mind if I do.

John: What she does is absolutely justified. Get out while you bloody well can.

Paul: That is what she does –

John: And what you leave behind you's just something that you've left behind.

Ringo: They're still talking about the song?

George: Not really.

Ringo: It's the mother I feel sorry for.

George: It's going to be painful whoever you are.

Paul: I think George is right. But that doesn't mean cruelty is a good thing. We all need to try and treat each other with decency and respect –

George: And compassion.

Paul: And love.

George: And mindfulness.

John: Mind your language.

Ringo: Mind the dog.

John: Ming the Magnificent!

Reporter: If I could just interject –

John: Watch it! This is me best jacket, sonny.

Paul: Go on.

Reporter: In the song, there's a man from 'the motor trade'. Is there any particular significance in that?

John: Look, mate, it's this – that poor girl's life is so bloody awful that she'll go off with the first pair of trousers that comes along.

George: They're his best trousers, too.

John: Old people just don't understand what it means to be young. They think they were young once, but they weren't. You can only *be* young. You can't look back and remember it and, sort of, *be* it again. Once it's finished it's finished, and you're practically finished, too, if you'd only admit it. You might as well get in the box and have them nail the lid down. Unless you grab hold of being young while you're young, you're never going to be able to do it later, after you've sensibly put away for your pension and collected your Green Shield Stamps.

Paul: People do their best, you know, in the circumstances they get given. I don't think you should blame them for being how or who they are or whatever.

Ringo: Rita Tushingham has nice legs, but not as nice as Julie Christie.

George: Sometimes, Ringo, old chum, I think you are the wisest of us all by quite a long chalk.

Ringo: Thank you, whoever you are.

Paul: Some of the people that hear the song are going to be all for the girl, and some of them will be feeling bad like for the parents, and –

John: Some of them will be right and some of them will be fools trying to stop time.

Paul: The song isn't there to make a judgement. It's to make people feel the situation, and then they can make up their own minds.

John: You're dead wrong.

Paul: Look, we're not talking about 'A Day in the Life' here. I think I know what –

John: I knew that girl. I saw her living in that house and dying every single moment in that terrible house.

Paul: It was in the papers. I read about her in the papers, and I thought about her, then I sat down and I wrote the song. On the piano, actually.

John: She was a lovely girl, not ordinary, and she didn't have one single piece of bright colour in her life. Not one single moment of joy or wonder. She lived twenty years of grey, behind those curtains. Like a sparrow covered in dust. And if she saw a little moment of brightness, and made a dash for it, then I'm all for her. I'm on her side completely, and against anyone who tries to stop her. I hate people who crush people just because they think they can. No one should be put in that position of absolute power over another human being – call them priest or father or whatever you want. That's the worst crime in the world, to kill another person's heart by killing their hopes. And that's what they were doing, those two, sitting there in their comfortable chairs and waiting up for her and passing eternal judgement on her for coming back smelling of port wine and aftershave. They'd tell her off for smiling, those skeletons. They're the sort who put plastic covers on their sofas and never take them off. And if they could've, they'd have put a cover on her. She did the right thing. Ran. Thousands didn't. They're still there now – sitting and having tea and biscuits with their prison guards.

Ringo: Rita's not in prison, is she?

George: Yet again!

Ringo: What did she do this time?

George (pretends to whisper in Ringo's ear): Psst-psst.

Ringo (in mock-shock): I hope they throw away the key.

Paul: I think what John's saying is, you know, like, you know –

John: Yes?

Paul: I agree with the part about freedom. I'm all for that. But when you just do what you want to do, there's always going to be some suffering left behind.

George (to Paul): Welcome, brother.

Paul: And if we could think about that, before we did anything, we'd all be a lot better off.

John: Some people don't think. Some people just kill.

Paul: 'She's leaving home' isn't about killing. It's about life.

There are five clear seconds of silence.

John: Look, right, I think it's a great song. Really. One of the best Paul's ever done. I'd like to pay sincere tribute to my partner of these – how long is it? – these twenty seven years. I'm going to have to look lively. Sheep up or shut out. He's no fool, that lad.

Paul: John helped with the chorus. You should ask about 'A Day in the Life'.

Ringo: I still can't believe that Rita murdered someone.

George: I have to put up with this all the time. Can you imagine?

Paul: Do you have another question?

Reporter: Yes –

John: As long as it's not about curtains.

AUTHOR BLURBS

Jenny Oliver is a great grandmother twice, who in the fifties discovered a locked ward and ECT. She spent the sixties married, pregnant and watching Jane Goodall on her first telly, wondering why child rearing was worse for women than for primates, she discovered why as a seventies feminist and inner city teacher before morphing into an eighties Indian guru sex and spirit woman-cum-adolescent and then travelling via personal growth to a nineties post-men kind of lesbian.

Wes Lee is originally from the UK, but currently lives in New Zealand. Formerly a lecturer in Fine Arts at Auckland University of Technology, she now focuses on the short story form. She has won a number of awards for her writing in the UK and in New Zealand, including *The BNZ Katherine Mansfield Award 2010* judged by Lloyd Jones, and *The Short Fiction New Writers Prize* (University of Plymouth Press). Her short fiction has appeared in literary journals and anthologies in the UK, New Zealand, Australia, and the US. More information can be found at her website: www.weslee.co.nz.

William Thirsk-Gaskill was born in Leeds in 1967. He studied chemistry at Liverpool University, where he associated with squatters and members of extreme left-wing splinter-groups and was a regular contributor to a fanzine called 'Dregs'. He spent a year in Poole, Dorset, where he was miserable, and 4 years in Glasgow, where he was happy. His current projects include a novel entitled 'The Companion', which is about a female android called Violet. He appears as a guest poet on *www.thehungrypoet.co.uk*. He lives in West Yorkshire with his partner and step-son. They have a cooker but no bathroom.

Tania Spooner studied at Oxford University and the Slade School of Art before designing for the theatre. Musical productions took her to Wiener Festwochen, the Young Vic and Winchester Jail, amongst other places. She now writes full-time. A Crack belongs to a collection of short stories. Her novel is currently a 20,000 word document.

Steven Maxwell has had stories published in *Horizon Review*, *Staple*, and *Dark Tales*, and was shortlisted for Legend Press's 'A Tale of Two Halves' novel-writing competition. He is currently studying for an MA in Creative Writing. His debut novel, *Band in Britain* (Kraken Press), will be published in 2012.

Ben Cheetham's stories have won awards and been shortlisted for several competitions, including Salt Publishing's Scott Prize for a full length short story collection. His literary fiction has appeared in *Various Authors* (published by The Fiction Desk), *The London Magazine*, *The Willisden Herald New Short Stories 3*, *Dream Catcher*, *Staple*, *Fast Forward: A Collection of Flash Fiction*, *Voice From The Planet* (published by Harvard Square Editions), *The Momaya Annual Review*, *The Chaffey Review*, *Swill* and numerous other magazines. Ben lives in Sheffield, UK, where he divides his time between writing and chasing around after his two-year old son.

Christian Stretton is the founder and editor of the flash fiction website And Figs Might Leaf. He is a regular contributor to Ready Steady Book and Rainy City Stories.

Holly Oreschnick is University of Huddersfield graduate. She has a deep interest in literature and poetry and has performed readings at many acclaimed venues around West Yorkshire. She has been a festival organiser for the Janet Beaumont Music and Drama Festival and has taught English at Mara Primary School in Tanzania. She is thrilled to be a part of the Grist Anthology.

Alexei Sayle is a British stand-up comedian, actor and author. He was a central part of the alternative comedy circuit in the early 1980s. In recent years he has turned to writing. He has written two short story collections and five novels. Sayle's latest book is called Stalin Ate My Homework and is a satirical memoir.

Mark Ellis is a liar, a wastrel and a thief. As Artistic Director of Collective Unconscious he is responsible for selling cheap, sexual experiences disguised as contemporary performance. A nasty piece of work, best to be avoided.

Jack Moss was born in Nottinghamshire in 1988, and currently lives in Leeds.

Joe Else is an impoverished London based refugee from local government, wishing she could find a way back into the 1950s , where she would live in an attic above a Soho drinking club with one gas ring and spend her time writing, learning languages and being clever over espresso. Born in 1969, if you really need to know.

Melvin Burgess is an acclaimed author of fiction for young adults. Junk was published in 1996 and immediately caused controversy. It is still one of the best known young adult fiction titles. His latest novel is called Kill Your Enemies.

Rosie Jones recently graduated from the University of Huddersfield with a First Class Honours Degree in English Language with Creative Writing and The Blue Touch Prize for Outstanding Writing. In her spare time, she loves to write short stories and is particularly inspired by the way in which tragedies test even the strongest relationships. She recently secured a job as a trainee researcher for Objective Productions in London as part of the Channel 4 Diversity Production Scheme.

Louis Malloy lives in Nottingham. He has had over forty stories published in a range of magazines and anthologies and has won various prizes, most recently first prize in the University Of Plymouth Short Fiction Competition. Publications his work has appeared in include *The Edinburgh Review*, *The New Writer* and *The Middlesex University Press Anthology*. Louis is also a novelist and a prolifically successful recipient of encouraging rejection letters.

Mason Henry Summers is currently working on his second novel whilst seeking a publisher for his first. Formerly a writer on film and cinema he now writes novels, short fiction and comment and is also working on a screenplay co-written with another writer. His work has been described as imaginative, funny, disturbing, relentless and certainly unique. He is co-organiser of Fictions Of Every Kind, the Leeds based open mic writer's event and showcase, where he comperes and occasionally reads. You can find examples of his work and contact details at www.monkeytwohands.com.

Dan Malach spends his days in the Manchester rain, weeping, but nobody notices because of the rain.

Suzi Lester was born in 1848. She fell through a rip in time and ended up in modern day Leeds, where she now works as a full time receptionist. In her spare time she likes eating, daydreaming and listening to Morrissey. She has a weakness for unusual notebooks and is constantly on the lookout for good vegan chocolate.

Stephen McQuiggan is from Northern Ireland and is a direct descendant of Judas Iscariot.

Susan Everett is an award-winning screenwriter and short story writer. Her first novel, *Crazy Horse*, was published by Route, and was a finalist in the Peoples Book Prize, 2010. Her short stories have appeared in several anthologies including *The Book of Leeds* (Comma), *Next Stop Hope* and *Compendium* (both Route). She wrote and directed the short film *Mother, Mine*, which played at 80 film festivals and won 16 international awards.

David T Hay is a freelance director in the TV industry and is more accustomed to writing for documentaries. Thankfully, the spells of unemployment that come with the profession give him the occasional opportunity to create some good, proper fiction.

John Todd was born in Hope in Derbyshire and now lives in Sutton Coldfield. He has been a local government officer and a lexicographer. 'The House Next Door' is his first published story.

David Pescod started writing jokes for BBC radio, whilst a student at The Royal College of Art. After running a greetings cards company he began writing prose in 2002, and 'Rising Laughter', a short story, was broadcast on BBC Radio 4. Other stories have been published in literary magazines and his first collection will be published by Route later this year. His story 'All Embracing' was adapted for a short film and selected for TCM's top twenty in 2009. He was selected for Norwich Writers Escalator scheme and recently awarded an Arts Council Grant to complete his first novel.

Glenis Burgess entered the Huddersfield Literature Festival competition under a pseudonym and, in the Peacock Lounge one evening sitting in an unknowing audience, could hardly stop herself screaming with delight when the shortlist was announced – she did go outside and yell a bit, though. She started writing in 2009 and the story featured in this anthology is about the third story she has written. She's had no (literary) reason to scream since the Huddersfield Literature Festival, mainly because she hasn't entered any other competitions. She is now in the Otley Courthouse Writers and Leeds Writers Circle, and is still writing, so watch this, and other spaces.

Toby Litt is best-known for writing his books – from *Adventures in Capitalism* to (so far) *King Death* – in alphabetical order; he is currently working on *L*. If he's known for anything else, it's occasionally constructing extremely technically restricted stories of a non-Oulipian sort for Radio 3's The Verb. His headfuckfiction™ story 'John & John' won the semi-widely-known Manchester Fiction Prize. His website is slowly going senile at www.tobylitt.com.